Northern Accents

A Collection of Short Stories

Matthew Drummy

Copyright ©2003
All rights reserved. Printed in the United States of America.
No part of this publication may be reproduced, stored in a
retrieval system, or transmitted, in any form or by any
means electronic, mechanical, photocopying, recording,
or otherwise, without the prior written permission of the author.

ISBN 1-58961-113-6

Published by PageFree Publishing, Inc.
8175 Creekside Drive
Portage, Michigan 49024
269-321-5030
www.pagefreepublishing.com
This is a work of fiction. Any resemblance to persons living or dead is purely coincidental.

Praise for *Northern Accents*

Matt Drummy is a marvelous writer, and *Northern Accents* is a stunningly original book of stories. In my twenty years of teaching, I have never seen a young writer so risk emotional injury in the composition of his stories. His characters are exposed, raw, and honest; his stories are relentlessly touching and inevitably moving.

—*Michael Martone, author of <u>The Blue Guide to Indiana</u> and <u>The Flatness and Other Landscapes</u>; Director of the Creative Writing Program at the University of Alabama-Tuscaloosa*

From *Northern Accents*

Moving down the aisle I thought about being a priest, or at least being *his* priest, washing his feet after a day at market, in Massachusetts yes this all did happen.

* * *

I grew up in Munising, on the Upper Peninsula of Michigan. Up Route 28 a bit on the left was a place called Christmas, which consisted of an ice cream stand, a huge plastic Santa Claus out front, and a broken-down gift shop across a side street. Out back of the gift shop was a black bear in a cage, and when I was a senior in high school, I got sick about that bear.

* * *

"My God," said Maggie as she drove, her voice weird and pure. "My God. It's like the Bible or something. My God, look what we . . . wrought. Or something."

* * *

Mary if I could have told you then I would have told you then, about sitting there like that, the crack you made inside me, the flipperflops and candymelt ooze, down near Daley Textile we skipped two o'clock flatrocks, when cuteyblue jacket wrapped my head 'round your lint-sweatered breasts and we giggled and moaned in the leathery early-morning purple-watered battery acid factory mishmash dump. . . .

About the Author

Matthew Drummy's stories have won the *Boston Magazine* Fiction Prize, the *Taproot Literary Review* Fiction Prize, and the best-story awards at both Harvard University and Syracuse University. He has published over a dozen stories in a wide variety of literary journals and is the Director of Writing Instruction at Woodbury College in Montpelier, Vermont. His passions include preserving the environment, ensuring health care for all, and saving the Montreal Expos. He lives in Strafford, Vermont, with Cricket, a seventeen-year-old cat.

Would You Like to Read More of Matt's Work?

If you enjoy this book and would like to be informed of Matt's future releases, please e-mail him at md89@post.harvard.edu. Thanks for your interest!

Acknowledgments

"Peggy Thinking Back" appeared in *Boston Magazine* in 1992. An earlier version, "Peggy Thinks Back," appeared in *How the Weather Was*, Ampersand Press, 1990.

"Bear in Christmas" was first published in *Taproot Literary Review*, 1996.

"Dairy Mart Kid" was first published in *Cactus Alley*, 1997.

"Peretuck, Early Seventies" was first published in *Calliope*, 1989.

"Marjorie" was first published in *Worcester Review*, 1998.

"Bay State Bombardier" was first published in *Texas Review,* 1998/1999.

"Self-Righteous Pedant" was first published in *Vermont Literary Review,* as "Self-Righteous Pedant, Shaker Heritage School," 1997.

"Peace Garden" was first published as "Peace Garden with Smarm, Cash" in *Salt Hill Journal*, 1993.

Cover Photo copyright 2003 by Sharon L. Denechaud.

Author Photo by Amy Zucker.

Interior Illustration, *Winter Bird #1*, copyright Laura Nugent, www.lauranugent.com.

Thanks and love to the following:

Amy.

Everyone at Woodbury: to the most wonderful students one could ever hope to teach, and to my co-workers, who have become my family.

My beloved supervisors and mentors: Rhonda, Gary, Woden, Susan, Muffie, Father Mulligan, and Steffi.

Everyone at OCDC, with extra-special thanks to Cindy, Steve, Senator Mark and Roberta, Ned and Vi, Bob, Mike, Linda, and all the candidates.

My writing teachers: Michael, Susan, Chris, Rilla, and Melanie.

The English Department at Vermont Technical College.

My family.

At Syracuse: Deb, Hackman and Susanne, Trish, Bill, Hekia, and Aron.

At Harvard: Rachel, Josh, Jonathan, Coley, Dave, Corey, Dinah, Emily, and Tom Corwin.

From way back: Dean, Peter, Alexia, Werner, and Scott Kahn.

Erin Todd, Patti Jamele, Elizabeth Marvin, Laura Nugent, Jeannine Greaves, Sharon Davenport, Diane Rivers, Karen

Schiff, Jacqui Messing, Heidi Lasher-Oakes, Laurie Reed, Galandrielle Richmond, Jeannie MacLachlan, Lisa Phillips, Joan Doubleday, Carol Babylon, Aneek Singh-Fisher, Barbara Coffino, Jasmine Lamb, Rob Wilson, Dave Smith, Sharon Denechaud, Mary Ellen Otis, Maura O'Neill, Shannon Budziak, Stephanie Rockwell, Lorraine Strang, Susan McGrath, Dawna Pederzani, Henry Payson, every living thing in Topanga Canyon, Andrew Stoll, Alice Bredice, Anna and Jessika Watkins, Donald Kleinschmidt, and Youppi.

I've left a bunch of people out because of space constraints, and I'm sorry. So many people helped me to get to the place where I needed to be in order to write. So many friends in workshops at Harvard, so many friends just talking about art with me, all over the country. I love you all.

For Joel
on behalf of Matt.
love,
Elizabeth
2009

For Amy

Table of Contents

Peggy Thinking Back 12

Bear in Christmas 22

Dairy Mart Kid 31

Dolphin 43

Peretuck, Early Seventies 49

Marjorie 58

Bay State Bombardier 77

Self-Righteous Pedant 92

Peace Garden 105

Apprentice 113

Peggy Thinking Back

It's Father Hernon I think about the most, but that doesn't mean he's important. I can't figure out what's important or what's only stuck in my mind. Father Hernon's just faded a little less than the rest, I guess, but it's all, my youthly times, they're all so far, so far, so far from my sick aim now it hurts to even shoot for them. I should have been a virgin, should have been a nun, because then maybe God would have come and shaken me and shouted, "Hey, Peggy, you're all right! You're all right the way you are!" But I got too normal, and He never came to me. I've heard other people say God has visited them. Maybe.

But Father Hernon. It wasn't his homilies or any of that stuff that sent me into some kind of glaze. As far as all that went, I suppose Jesus Christ could have walked into five o'clock Mass and I still would have gotten a creaking headache from the heat, the wood, and Ma's perfume. No, no, it was more seeing Father in the supermarket on a rainy Tuesday all collared and glasses, and buying just vegetables from what I could tell, altogether holy it seemed to me I visioned a bunch of priests sitting around boiling broccoli and chopping lettuce and talking about green priestly things, and here was Father Hernon supplying the feast like the angel he was, well maybe not an angel, but I saw all of this in the middle of Pilgrim

Supermarket, as I peeked at him from between the limes and around the toilet paper, as I stood there in bright lights Muzak and stared at him, do you know that saintliness did seem possible? Moving down the aisle I thought about being a priest, or at least being *his* priest, washing his feet after a day at market, in Massachusetts yes this all did happen.

Father Hernon came by our house sometimes, because they sent the youngest priest out to smile at the old people. And my grandmother was really old. So Father would sit with her wrinkles and her bedroom smell for a bit—oh God I'm being cruel and I'm gonna end up like that myself soon enough but yeah, that's the way she was—he'd sit with her and then after a pointless while he'd come out to the kitchen and melt in quietly with me and the tea. I didn't have a father, and maybe my mother had asked Father Hernon to talk with me once in a while, but he didn't have to spend the time with me that he did. Did I have the right to think that he liked being there with me, that he liked having a minute off with a girl who wasn't pretty but who at least talked to him and didn't hang up on his being a priest? I guess no one has such a right, because it's vanity to think you're worth anything. And you know I've got to say that Father Hernon, if he's still alive, probably doesn't even remember me, because he only came over once in a while. He just got big in my mind and somehow stays lodged in there as Time runs by, and, you know, I have to say that sometimes I feel like he's the only thing in my life that makes it seem it ever mattered.

And even if this is all nonsense I do know that Father Hernon loved the tea I made for him, no one can deny that. "I love my tea, Peggy, thank you for my tea." I remember looking at his matted-down hair clinging blondly to his forehead and thinking, "He's the only priest ever that didn't have black hair." Father Hernon with his runny nose.

"Father, they might be damming up the river in Feynard."

"Damming?"

"Yeah, you know, damming. With the bricks and all."

"Oh! Mmm, mmm, I know, I know. A lot of . . . people are concerned."

"Yeah, the kids don't care, the kids don't care in school, but all their parents'll be running out of jobs, they'll care," me with my stupid fourteen-year-old radical politics. "You think it's gonna shut us down, shut the, Rossi on the news said the whole town'll go kaput."

He was silent for a long minute, I thought he was wandering but he was probably thinking. I couldn't help, I blurted, "Father, never mind, forget it, there's something else. That story about Jesus cursing the fig tree. You know that one?"

He laughed a bit. "Yeah."

"I didn't mean to think you didn't," I said, not wanting to insult him, "I just thought, you know, there's so many Bible stories, *I* can't keep them straight. . . ."

"Don't worry about it, Peggy. I forget a lot of things."

"Well anyway, that story, we talked about it in catechism class a while back, and . . . I just didn't get it at *all*, I didn't get why."

"Why what?"

"Well . . . why did he curse the fig tree?"

"Uh. . . ." And another eternal pause and this time I waited. "To show that . . . well actually, you're supposed to need more than faith."

And I didn't want to argue with him, because he was a Father and a ragged one at that, but that word *faith* rang a bell and I could never just shut up, I said, "Miss Martelli said in catechism all you need is faith, that's all you need and then you can do whatever you want." I was hoping he'd say, "damn that Miss Martelli, she's spreading lies," because I didn't like

Miss Martelli, she was pretty, she didn't have any freckles, she dated my cousin.

But Father just said, "I don't know. What to say. About that story, and . . . faith." He gave a tiny laugh and shook his head once. "Really, *I don't know*. Isn't that funny. I don't know how to figure everything out. Maybe I shouldn't be a priest." And he went and dumped his tea out into the sink.

Two Saturdays later in church Father got to give the homily. There were a lot of men from the mill at that Mass, because they worked midnight-to-eight shift and weren't about to go to nine o'clock Sunday Mass. And so normally they just kind of slumped there and dozed, on their wife's shoulder if they were lucky. But this Saturday Father Hernon, who no one ever really thought about twice if you want me to be honest, Father Hernon gets up there and says, "I know a lot of you must be concerned about the mill possibly closing down from the dam up in Feynard. And I was thinking about this and I talked to a very good friend, a very special person, and it's one of you out there." My stomach got sick and jumpy at the same time, like they said it did for the Beatles or someone like that. And Father Hernon goes on to say, "I don't know why they're closing the mill down. It's just like I don't know why Jesus cursed the fig tree, in Mark Chapter 11 which I just read to you. Some things, a lot of things, they just don't make any sense. No sense, no sense. Nonsense world." And there wasn't as much dozing then, a lot of people were sitting up taking notice, for maybe the first time in their lives. Because ordinarily the priests never talked about the mill, and never said stuff like *no sense*; they just droned the same sayings week after week. And me, I was all awake and earpricking, because I knew that Father Hernon was speaking of him and me in the kitchen, and he'd put it all together and although he still hadn't figured it out I thought, "Now this is what a priest should be, *yes*, this is what a priest should be, *damn* yes, this is...." And then he said, "In fact, most things don't make sense. I'm not even sure there's any reason for me to be up here. Sometimes I wonder how important it is for *you* to be here, to take the time.... Probably you should, but I'm just not *sure*. You see, it's a strange world, tough to prove anything, understand anything. Hard to figure out the angles . . . the angels...." And the place was buzzing and church seemed like a movie theater, everyone wondering where Father Hernon was going next, and the bald guy in front of me, whose name I never could remember, leaned to another guy and said, "This joker's flipped, they'll have him out of here in a week." And the other guy said, "Yeah, but Cripes, it's makin' the time go by quick anyway," and through all this I started to think, "Oh my God, oh my God, they're going to send Father Hernon away," and it was worse than losing anything else I could think of.

But after he stood there looking down, not at the Bible, not at the pulpit, just down, I think Father Hernon decided to save himself. Because he went into the thing about faith and how you've gotta have it, and we could just about hear Father McCannon and Father Houle heaving big sighs off in their back room, all seemed calm again, only inside of me something kept spinning circles for the whole rest of the Mass.

And while we were milling around on the front steps afterwards, some kid's First Communion or whatnot, there's a crowd around Father Hernon, buzzing, backslapping, and all of a sudden Mrs. Cowley runs up screaming, "You're not a priest, you're a . . . *farce*, the way you ran that Mass." And Father seemed to shrink, his sad face paling, the impossible dark stains on his black cassock underarms, the crowd surging like a Thanksgiving football game, Father Hernon gone through a side door, Mrs. Cowley sneering, "You'll never see that priest again, he'll never ruin our Mass again, we'll have him out of here!" and me crying, believing her.

But Father Hernon stayed, even quieter than before. They shut him up—didn't want any of those scenes ever again—but for some reason he stayed on, listening to confession every once in a while and the rest of the time holed up in the rectory: "studying," Miss Martelli told me. And I suppose I began to forget. You have to forget, otherwise you'll go batty. I think.

And they dammed the river and everyone lost jobs, but the world didn't end. Some people died, some people left, some stayed and found jobs an hour's ride away, but . . . the world didn't end. We had a priest up from the South for a few weeks, *he* said the world would end, but it didn't.

And my grandmother, she died, and they sent an even younger priest over to do the old people thing, he came to see Grandma lying there in her last seconds, Father I-Can't-Remember with wire glasses. It wasn't the same as Father Hernon but I couldn't blame the guy.

And finally Father Hernon showed up one day when I was sixteen. I wasn't about to ask him about his not seeing me for so long, because he looked like wasted dough, milky drops dripping out of his nose.

But I lost all of that teenaged holdback strength when I went to the stove and the whistle and tea leaves came together and memory and life is sad, damn it, damn it, damn it *all* sometimes.

"Father, you haven't been here in two whole years, what do you think—"

"I'm sorry." And I guess that was enough to shut me up, I was lost to him all over again.

Father Hernon was there for my mother, she was on her own kind of prolonged deathbed, though I didn't know it at the time. They'd told Jacky and me that she'd just taken too much of the wrong medicine, nobody's fault. Things just happen.

Anyway, back then my mother was a philosopher. Most people sniggered when I'd say that, but that day when Father Hernon returned I told him about hearing my mother on the phone right before she got sick, talking about my wandering lost older brother, she was saying, "If they could die when they were eighteen, there'd be no war. If they'd die when they were fifteen, maybe there wouldn't even be any of these ... drugs. But they live, and I've got all this shit, and ... I'm not about to love them for the sake of loving them." And I said to Father Hernon, "There's got to be some sort of philosophy in all of that."

"Yes, I suppose there is, but ... well, how do you feel when you hear her say something like that?" Father Hernon always asked the right questions, it made me excited.

"When I, when I, when I heard her say those things, I felt like I should do good."

"Why?"

"Well, I," my mind racing all over to be worthy of Father Hernon, "because I suppose Ma is, Ma's right, I mean ... well, Ma let me, I came out of her, and you've got to defend something like that, you've got a responsibility to a Ma, I think," for weeks after that I thought about my mother and wondered whether I really did owe her anything, and you see that's *it*, that's the way it was with Father Hernon, he hardly ever said anything but I always found myself discovering selfly things just by talking to him.

"Well, if you're *trying* to be good, I think you'll do okay, unless your good is someone else's bad, I don't know. I *don't know*." And he must have seen me falter and confuse a bit, because he added, "Just be good, Peggy, keep being good."

And I was a good girl then, I think, back in high school, I didn't have much choice I suppose, with big-frame glasses and Irish freckles bunched round my nose, but I'm sure there were a couple boys out there wouldn't have minded making me bad. But I stayed good I think because it was scary to be bad, to be dancing and drinking and tales of wet cigarettes by the faraway shore, I'm not sure if it was because of God or if I was just shy, but I decided to stay with my soft bedcloth nights with Ma and Auntie murmuring in the kitchen and little Jacky clean from his bath and snoring through our cardboard walls,

but then ten hours later was homeroom in the bright light threatening through the wide windows that looked out on the football field, oh all those names that I cannot forget though it's been untold years, Donato and Medeiros and McDowell, Massachusetts won't let you forget, and Father Hernon working, studying, dispensing grace, two miles away but it seemed like a million from that school, school was not home but school was real and they all told me, deskmate and counselor and the other priests when I asked them, they said school was where I should be me and grow up, so I tried. And I remember so many of them saying, even one of the priests, that to be drunk was to be me.

But I got drunk just once in those high school times, at my cousin's party, danced all around. I felt the sweat everywhere, on my eyebrows, on my armpit bristles, between the skin and the sweater was sweat some more. Bruce Freeman, he was considered ugly and just third string, so he must have said what the hell, he called me over and we tried to dance together and I was just terrible, turning in on my knees, but he got me on the couch just about in front of everyone, all eyes on my body slipping rolling crashing embarrassing into antique smashing coffeetable, those were the things that made me flee to Father Hernon, who *never* told me I had to party or drink, those were the things that kept me all ponytailed and pale, those were the things that made me alone still today, regardless of how normal I've tried to get, but oh, keep going, keep going,

I left Father with a squeeze of the hand, I was off to some college where the people were tanned, and when I returned for Thanksgiving that year Father was gone, sent to convert the heathen of Peru. I went back to school early and a-dazed, and I walked in the door and saw my roommate Janet doing something that I will never forget, between two men and a bottle of wine, and it seemed at that moment as I shrunk huddled to the space between my bed and the wall that I was now an adult, because these groaning-type things were only whispered of around the playgrounds and corridors, and I decided that I must grow up, so I closed my eyes and grabbed the bottle from amongst the flesh and glugged it down with all the pleasure of gasoline, and as my mind left me and I whined something about "I wanna join in," Janet said rather kindly I suppose, "You can't, Peggy, you've still got braces on your teeth, you might hurt one of the guys."

That night I lay half-under my bed dreaming of Father Hernon. And my dream wasn't what you might want, it wasn't fingers inside and priestly sex but rather it was Father Hernon as he always was, sweating, pained, but nice to me forever, and when I woke up in the early morning of bodysmells and barely-clothed I went to the bathroom and thought of slitting my wrists but "suicide is murder" he'd said once and murder is Hell and Hell is the flesh melting and dripping off of my bones, anyway I went back home for good about a week later, and sometimes looking back looking now at age forty-five ready to die like Ma and Grandma, I wish that there weren't no Catholic and there weren't no Father and there weren't no me.

But Father wherever you are don't hate me, I don't like thinking about these things, I guess I do it because if I don't I'm just running away from it all, and that isn't right either.
Mm-hmm.
So anyway, to get this all done and on with my life—
Some kids made fun of me once in a while because I loved Father Hernon so much and because I wasn't afraid to talk about it, and it bothered me when they'd say "you're supposed to have friends your *own age*, Peggy," and there were times when I hated the whole deal, but I think I loved Father just because he loved me so much, no one ever understands this because they say that a priest is *supposed* to love you, but I couldn't help my feeling and still can't, no matter what all the shit that came afterwards, I think God wants us to keep our feelings if they're good ones, and I wish I could have held his hand forever, because he took care of me and patted me and I will always remember that I was a Catholic girl on the Sunday back woodroads of New England where once with my Father we rolled through piney fields of pumpkin and turkey and Christmas Tree, we could have brought home a different prize for every month it seemed, for the rectory, for my Mom, right then at that . . . moment . . . I thought I couldn't be happier, because all was life and life was quite . . . benign, you know,

and Father talked with the Dads and pumpkinsellers, and those long-ago farmstand dwellers with sacks for shirts, they all made quiet noise about the football game while I myself in the growing places went about the serious business of tree-compare and pumpkin pick-and-choose, oh God it was my sarsaparilla heyday, hey-hey, gee-tars on the radio, hey-ho, it was 1968, I was alive, and I didn't
                even
                know it.

Bear in Christmas

I grew up in Munising, on the Upper Peninsula of Michigan. Up Route 28 a bit on the left was a place called Christmas, which consisted of an ice cream stand, a huge plastic Santa Claus out front, and a broken-down gift shop across a side street. Out back of the gift shop was a black bear in a cage, and when I was a senior in high school, I got sick about that bear.

If he had stood up, he would have been a little taller than me. But he never stood up, he just sat on all fours by the narrow tin chute leading into his cage from the outside. Matted fur covered his body, except for a pale pink bald spot behind his left ear, and a patch of foamy drool circling his mouth. He had a lump of pus on his right jowl, and it shook when he rattled the chute with a paw, which he did whenever someone walked up to the cage. The rattling meant he wanted food. To feed him, you bought stale doughnuts and Danish from the French lady in the gift shop. She called it "Bear Food."

Even when I'd feed him, he'd just keep looking down at the ground, which was dirty with his own leavings. Through the bear, I saddened about everything.

Now let's be honest, football players aren't supposed to sadden. But after practices I'd go to fluorescent Dairy Queen and spew all this stuff to Maggie, who was older, about thirty-five. I knew her from the factory where I worked the line on weekends. People figured she must be Miss Kickass, being the lady in the factory with the nail gun and all, but people are full of crap.

"I can't take it anymore," I told her one day. "I can't even eat my rings." The onion rings laughed at me from their cardboard carton centered perfect on the Formica top. "You shouldn't, you know, have to live a life like that, in a six-foot cage with nowhere to go. I mean, he can only take one step in any direction. He'd be better off dead." Saying that made me feel even more pukish and briny; saltburgers were coming up from the previous night's DQ.

"Yeah, I know." Maggie rarely *showed* any pain that she felt. She didn't show lip corners, either, just sat with the same turned-in mouth and listened.

"I'm truly," I said, "inside, I'm sick. I don't see why life is—"

"Okay, stop. Cut it out. Look . . . we know it's not right, okay. The bear—he should be in the woods. I don't believe he's happy in that cage." She spoke with an accent from Quebec, to which she eventually returned, and her weird pauses and swallowed-up *o*'s reminded me without fail of my long-dead father. "But what can you do," she mumbled. "Life is life."

"Yeah, life is life, but still that bear must be lonely, I'm not kidding now—he never sees another bear." I thought further of little kids who would stop with their parents and see the bear sick and ragged, and of the parents deciding to laugh it off, "Oh, look at the stupid bear," kids laughing because parents are laughing, kids becoming parents, world screwing itself over unending. "Look," I said, "I'm sorry to bring you down, I should be happy with you. It's just that I can't tell anyone else. I can't tell anyone at school, because no matter what I say at school, Selkirk finds out." Selkirk was the fullback, team captain who used to be my friend before girls and beer were invented. "If I told Selkirk about the bear, bastard'd be like, 'Hey, football players are supposed to *shoot* bears! Don't be a faggot!' Selkirk, yeah—"

"Oh, the hell with Selkirk, the hell with everything about him. I know his father, they're a pair. Frigging . . . jam everything into a box, and if something doesn't fit, they frigging . . . crush it." This was a lot more feeling than she usually showed, and she seemed embarrassed. She played with the straw in her freeze. "Look, whatever. Selkirk, he doesn't matter, he's not even close to mattering, Mick."

"Yeah, I know, I know, he doesn't matter. I know. But it's easy for you to say, Maggie. Floating above everything."

"I don't float! Don't float. Okay? I just don't . . . let it bother me. But I don't float."

"Yeah, all right, I know you don't float. I know. Hey, gee, I guess I know everything, actually, no point in talking about it."

Around about November, when it was so cold I couldn't bend my fingers, I started to hate football as much as the rest. I was halfway good at it, but I'd begun to realize that I didn't want to be with people I didn't like. I especially didn't want to run five-below dummy drills with them. And plus it was just wrong to be near Selkirk.

So I found myself skipping skull sessions to go see the bear. The links on his cage were iced over, so on sunny days I saw him through a glazed rainbow that put me in mind of God. But his wheezing tinny moans told me he was still sick. God wasn't there, it was a fake-out.

I knew the crap food couldn't be good for him, but he asked for it, so I always bought it and slid it down the chute.

He'd scrapple it all up, first off the ground, then tongue-to-steel for the sticky bits. Then he'd rattle the chute again.

I should have just pounded on that withered French lady inside the shop and said, "Give me the key to the cage, lady, I want to let the bear out!" But she was just stupid and nice. She barely knew how to talk, for Christ's sake, and I didn't want to hurt her, either. So I'd hint around, "Is that bear okay in there, ah, do you think?"

"Oh, he's a good bear, oh yeah, a big fuzzy bear. Kids like him!"

"Right. Yeah, I like him too, but . . . I mean, do you think he gets enough exercise? I mean, do you ever let him out?" Hoping she'd reassure me, say, "Oh yeah, we take him to Hiawatha Forest for a run on the weekends, he plays with his bear friends!"

But instead she just said, "Couldn't let the bear out! He'd run away!" And she laughed.

And goddamn I laughed, too, because I didn't want to be rude to her. Meanwhile the bear was out freezing and rotting in the back.

Near Thanksgiving I dreamed about the lump on the bear's jowl. It grew and grew, then burst. The bear was dead. White maggots streamed out of him.

The next day, before practice, Selkirk and his crew decided to shave all the hair off this little freshman cornerback's body, in an effort to make him more a part of the team. They strung him up by the lockers while I stood to the side, and Selkirk turned to me and screamed, "Can't you fucking get off your high horse and join in?" And meanwhile Coach Meezer was sitting with the radio and the assistants in his office pretending not to hear any of it, and the whole horrible cramped locker room was fire-drilling with the freshman's screams, and so me I just busted out, thinking for a moment of freedom.

But there was no freedom in my ratty tiny car, just broken 8-track and nothing but crap on the radio. Couldn't escape, kept seeing that kid's bloody anus, kept seeing the distance between me and it. Kept seeing me.

Maggie was still at work, so I cruised with nowhere to go, ending up on Becket Hill. I looked out on my brown city stuck there on the shore, wondering even then, I suppose, if I'd ever leave it. And wondering why it had been arranged for me to feel the way I did about bears, instead of wanting to kill them, like my teammates wanted, like all normal, healthy Munising males wanted. Life would have been a lot easier that way, God knows.

After about an hour I collided with Maggie at the DQ. "I don't have any goddamn answers, Maggie, I need answers now, not just your little . . . words and agreements and disagreements. I want to be steady like you, I need you to tell me what to do—"

"I'm not steady—"

"Whatever! Goddamn it, why don't you help me? I mean, what the hell good are you?"

I don't think I'd ever said anything like that to her before. She just stared at the empty napkin holder.

"Look, Maggie, that bear's got more of a right than Selkirk, *fucking* Selkirk—"

"Will you watch your language, please?" It was Mrs. Mikulson, big glasses and frosted hair, with her grandkids in the booth across the way. Out for a DQ treat with the grandkids and here they're confronted with some raving nutcake pounding the table. The little girl, name escaping me, had huge, brown, wet eyes. I'd made her eyes wet.

"Sorry, Mrs. Mikulson."

So I tried to talk lower. "Look, Maggie, I've got my stomach in my mouth here, I got like . . . burning. I can't stop thinking about the bear."

"I want to help, Mick. You know, you know I do, really. Sometimes I feel sick, too. Some things, though, maybe you just can't let them bother you, you know. . . . I mean, you can't just think about that bear the rest of your life. There's a lot of bad things in the world, you can't let them all bother you," she trailed off.

"Oh, for Christ's sake, it's your same old crap, I mean, of *course* they should bother you! What do you think you're supposed to do, ignore them? I think of him there in the cold dark, alone forever, freezing, man, he's got a bald spot," and there I was, a bad joke, crying in the DQ, a football player crying in front of Mrs. Mikulson and snotty alleycat girl behind the counter and any other Munising type. Maggie shoveled me outside to the snow.

Where I cried on her shoulder, on a creased wool jacket that chafed, but she did pat my back, kind Maggie. I should have realized right then that all you can hope for is someone who halfway cares. It's just stupid blindness to expect more. I mean Maggie was more than my screwed-up self will ever have again, as far as I can see. But in those days I wanted more, I wanted to make wrong things right, and I cried when I couldn't. And Maggie held me for a minute of my time, even with the people from inside looking out.

Finally she said, "Okay, we'll do something. We'll do something to help the bear. Come on, get in the truck."

My sickness shifted out, and though I knew the shift couldn't last, time at least ran slow for a bit while I tried to think. Maggie drove us, silent, in her overheated pick-up, the million-degree cab making me sweat, up that eight-mile stretch of nothing but deer signs and Lake Superior glinting through the dusky woods on the right. I started to get burning sick again, owing I guess to not knowing how we were going to help the bear, and afraid Maggie didn't know either.

So I asked. I could ask. "How are we going to help the bear?"

And she just said, "Well, we'll let him go, Mick, we'll let him go." She squeezed my neck a bit. "We'll saw the lock open, I've a hacksaw in the back. Cool?"

"What'll happen to the bear?"

"I suppose he'll make for the woods. Instinct, right?"

Then we were in Christmas, and it was dark. We parked across the little street, behind Santa Claus, and walked to the overgrown backyard where the cage was. The bear wasn't expecting us, he wasn't at the chute; we could hear him in the corner trying to get up, and then we saw him crawling over to us. He pawed at the chute.

I watched Maggie take to the lock, her messy, wispy hair spilling out of her cap and down the back, hair always too long for the factory rules. I was scared the French lady would hear the screeching saw, but the wind was pretty heavy and blocked it out.

After a bit Maggie said, "I think that's it, the thing's pretty rusty." She wrestled with the gate and it came open. We stood, sweat freezing on our faces, and nothing between us and the bear, and we waited for something to happen.

But the bear wouldn't move. He just sat, shivering and fuzzy and huge.

"Go, bear, go!"

"There you go, kid, there you go!"

He didn't get it.

Then Maggie was saying, "Jeez, what do we do? I mean . . . maybe jam the door shut and leave?"

And right away I knew, *not back to that life, no way.* And I knew also that if I went into that cage to pull the bear out, he might kill me. Might. I simply didn't know what bears thought, knew, or needed. But I did ponder this: that maybe going into the cage, if I just let it happen, would be the right thing for once. So I waited. For maybe ten seconds, something.

Then I was in the cage, on the back of the bear, my hands grabbing a roll of fat around his neck, his hair crinkly, like maybe a porcupine, and smelling like an exploded toilet, but I hugged my bearfriend, planted my feet and leaned into him towards the open gate, he was snuffling and warbling, making noises like pushing a heavy wood table across linoleum, I was all in there with the bear, just me and Bear, and then he wasn't there anymore. I was on the bottom of the cage where stuff was soft but the smell wasn't as bad because the bear was gone.

Bear didn't kill me.

When I looked up, he was limping around the junky yard, favoring the right front paw, and Maggie was shouting, "Hey! Hey!" She was pointing at the house, where a light was on in the window. We bolted, cut through Santa's legs, and jumped into the truck. Last I saw of the bear, he was over near a row of bushes that led to the woods.

"My God," said Maggie as she drove, her voice weird and pure. "My God. It's like the Bible or something. My God, look what we . . . wrought. Or something."

I slept okay that night; I thought about how the bear was now naturalized, no matter what else. And I thought sleepily of being in the cage, and of the way things worked out.

But how they really worked out was predictable, I guess. And I'm sure Selkirk laughed in his Schlitz about it. Because it came on the radio the next morning on my way to school, making my throat go slow and thick. A weird little accident up near Christmas, an escaped bear smashed to death by a semi.

Meaty little bear bits sticking to Route 28. Crows picking at them in between the traffic. And then the French lady's voice in my car, getting interviewed, "My poor bear, someone put him loose. My poor dead bear. Who would do such a thing?"

Not me, God.

Dairy Mart Kid

The summer between my freshman and sophomore years at Brown University I found myself working the graveyard shift at a convenience store in East Providence, near where my Dad and I lived in Riverside. Brown hadn't taught me quite yet about internships and networking and such, and thus I was stuck in the same type of job I'd had throughout high school.

But somehow, working the midnight shift was rapturous, as long as I didn't think about the pathetic nature of it all. I had total autonomy in my Dairy Mart Kingdom until boss Jeannie arrived at eight in the morning. And when I'd get home, Dad would be off to work already, and I'd bury myself in bed and fall asleep with the morning comics. You know, I wouldn't mind doing it today; it's too bad Dairy Mart pays minimum wage and isn't prestigious.

This lack of prestige occasioned much glee amongst the truckers, cops, and various loners who made up my clientele. "Frigging Brownie genius working at a Dairy Mart! Ha! Local boy made *real* good!" But the dominant customer was Sludge Man, and he didn't hassle me.

He trucked sludge up and down Route 6, which twisted thence all the way to California, though I don't think Sludge Man ever made it past Connecticut. He took a weird, prodding interest in me, I suppose because I let him eat stuff for free, but also because I bothered to listen to him hurl slurs at the world: blacks, gays, non-hunters, "people like that." I maneuvered and danced around his venom stream, keeping my feet clean, convincing myself that my subject-shifting remarks and feigned laughter kept me morally grounded while simultaneously maintaining Sludge Man's respect for me. Achieving this balance, I felt whole: both Brownie and Local.

One night, about the middle of July, Sludge Man challenged me about Trisha, a huge woman-girl from Cranston who always came in and bought Camels near the end of Sludge Man's stint, around 3:30. "I'm telling you she's a cheap hooker. Why don't you palm the till, X out a few sales, and do a quickie in the back? It's all you, kid."

Sludge Man's vulgar suggestion verbalized a visceral fantasy that I'd been indulging just before sleep each morning. I didn't know whether or not Trisha was a prostitute, but she talked about sex a lot and excited me painfully, with her foul mouth, sweat stains, and smeared green mascara.

Sludge sensed an opening. "Trisha likes you, dude, she wants you, she thinks you're nice. I bet she'll give you a discount. What you got to lose?"

Trisha smiled at me once in a while, but no one had ever *wanted* me, in the way Sludge meant. I was just a pale-faced nothing with good grades.

I had to answer him. "Well, you ask what I could lose? I could lose my girlfriend, maybe. I shouldn't cheat on her."

"Your girlfriend's in New York, for Chrissakes! And she ain't hanging with you forever, kid, believe me."

Sludge Man knew everything. Leah was indeed summering in acting school in Greenwich Village. Sophisticated San Franciscan with foreign oniony breath and oversized lips, she'd decided for a while at Brown that I was delightfully earthy and local, but was now perceiving the redundant downside of said qualities and becoming "concerned about our relationship."

"I could also lose my health," I countered, pondering the germs that must have infested the wanton Trisha. But Sludge Man shot me his incredulous look. "Hey, you really think I'm stupid, don't you, Sludge Man? Well, I am! Just because I go to Brown, you know, doesn't signify...." I was stuck between normal Rhode Islandish and my Brown voice.

Sludge Man wasn't listening anyway. "Look, let me show you something," he said, walking around to the Secret Land behind the counter, where according to Jeannie Rules no customers were ever supposed to go. As I labored to, let's see, devise a conversational technique that would communicate the fact of Sludge Man's transgression to him while simultaneously indicating that I didn't actually care about said transgression, he took action and grabbed a black three-pack box of Ramses condoms. "Know what these are?"

"I sell them!" I laughed.

"That don't mean you know what they are. Anyway, kid, you use these, and you're all set. 'Lubricated!'" he read, and stuffed the box in the breast pocket of my blue Dairy Mart shirt. "Tonight's the night, kiddo."

We waited for Trisha. I wanted the moment to last, the *before* moment wherein I could live all of the possibilities with none of the consequences. The moment expanded, as I recall, and became briefly whole. Taking our snacks, rhythm at 3:30, crunching the lightly greased Munchos, slurping the Crush, then I was stocking the beans, rotating the milk, listening to the sports, as Sludge Man slumped against the wall. Oil Can Boyd was going nuts with the Red Sox that year, in and out of jails and hospitals. When the report ended, I flicked the switch to "Tape" and some wild jazz fusion filled our senses, richocheting through the Kingdom.

Finally, Sludge Man burned out on the intensity; he walked over to the boom box, turned the music off, and said, "Fucking nigger. Boyd. That's what it is. That's why he acts like that. He's a nigger."

"Uh-huh. Well, he's also just a weird guy." I couldn't tell him that I wanted to be quiet again and listen to the fusion. And that my best buddy at Brown was black, and on and on.

"All niggers are weird," he said. "Some of them are faggots, too."

I gave a little laugh.

"Lot of faggots over to Brown," he commented.

"Yeah. Yeah, I kind of keep to myself, avoid all that."

Trisha appeared, waddling and sweating. She aimed for the Big Hair look but sweated so much that it was always an unruly silver-brown mess, sticking to her forehead in locks. Her messy massiness excited me, her realness. The fact that maybe she liked me. Wanted me.

"Hey," she wheezed.

"Hey," I said, behind the counter.

Sludge Man elbowed me.

"You want Camels?" I asked her.

Sludge Man snorted, then drifted to the soda cooler.

"Yeah," she said, glaring at Sludge Man.

"Yeah." I gave them to her, didn't ask for money. Her pudgy rubbery pinky nubbled mine briefly.

"I just went down on this guy over to Taunton Avenue—he turned out to be a real asshole. He wasn't even a good time." Such Trisha Talk gave me a juvenile tingle in the groin.

"Yeah," I said.

She looked around. "Sludge Man says you're a weirdo. Where you from again?" she asked, for maybe the eleventh time that week. She was struggling to open the package of Camels, and I noticed as her eyes narrowed that they were black, green, and brown, mutt eyes.

"Uh, Riverside."

"Riverside! And you go to Brown," which became *Bvown* with the Cranstonese. "That *is* weird."

"Yeah, well . . . I got a scholarship."

"They gave you money?"

"Yeah."

She nodded. It was boring.

"And you're from Cranston," I confirmed, for the one hundredth time. Sludge Man, behind her and by the magazines, was sticking his finger down his throat.

"Yeah, yeah, you know that," she said. "Do you like this job?" She was smoking now. She wasn't supposed to, according to Jeannie Law.

"It's all right, you know. Uh . . . my dad doesn't like that I have it."

"What?" The non-sequitur had woken her slightly.

"Dad, uh . . . you know, I mentioned to him that my roommates at Brown were in, like, Wall Street and Europe for the summer—"

"Sounds like bullshit," she puffed.

"Yeah, well, I think Dad thinks that after a year at Brown I should *own* the Dairy Mart, you know. Or at least manage it." A little more. "Dad says I'm a *goddamn lazy fake-smart son*." I felt a little like crying: happy that she was listening, disgusted that it made me happy.

"Uh-huh. Well, you know, shit, you could have worse problems. I mean your life could be tougher, right?"

"Well . . . no question, yeah."

"But screw your dad. You know, you're all right." And that felt wholly nice, both sweet and raunchy. "A nice guy, not like Sludge Man here."

"Fuck you!" fired Sludge Man, over by the hot dog warmer.

"Ha! You wish." And then Trisha turned back to me. "But you're all right. Maybe you *should* be the manager."

Sludge Man was making frantic gestures, near the candy racks now. The man was everywhere. He was jamming a can of Cheez Whiz into a palm, over and over again, looking at me, then at the can, thrusting his face forward, trying to send signals.

"Thanks a lot," I said, "you're all right, too," and then I laughed to ford off the sentimentality of it all.

"Yeah. I'm going to grab a coffee," said Trisha. She headed to the far corner.

Sludge Man surged and leaned towards me over the counter. He smelled like a dog-track bathroom: ammonia and beer.

"The time is now, kid."

"Yeah. Yeah. Whence the ammonia, Sludge Man?"

"The time is now."

"Uh-huh." Nowhere to go. *And maybe that's good*, I thought. "Well, what the hell am I going to do? Close the shop?"

"I'll cover the register for you. No one's going to come in, anyway!" He leaned back, squirted some Whiz into his dirt-caked hand, and began to lick.

Something pre-Leah, pre-Brown kicked in. Some lonely teenage thing about giving anything to just once find out what illicit sex was like, given all the hoopla surrounding it. Something like that, because all I could want at that moment was to be sweaty, slimy, and enveloped by huge Trisha and her fat rolls.

My only concern was Lottery Woman, who was due soon for her third and final appearance of the shift. Bad teeth and balding, the most sad-making person I ever knew. Even profit-margin Jeannie had told me to go easy on her, "don't let her buy more than nine tickets a night, three per visit." She never won more than five bucks, and even then she just wanted to use the money to buy more tickets and get more depressed. I didn't know what Lottery Woman would do if she walked in and found me not there.

"Are you going to do it or what?" Sludge Man hissed. "Are you going to let some rich Frisco New York bitch twirl you around? What is it, you too good for a Cranston girl? Too good for a fat girl? You ain't so—"

"No! No! Actually, I'd love to go in the back with her." There. "It's just, you know, I do have a responsibility to Leah, and it's . . . just—"

"You're scared!"

"Maybe."

He put his arm around me. "Look, kid, you go for it. She's not going to bite you! And your girlfriend—hey, if you really think that freaking snob's not screwing around on you—"

"All right!" All right. "All right, Sludge Man." Something big seemed about to happen, but I was so confused by my body chemicals and this looming beard wanting me to have sex with this other person. Why? "Why," I said hazily, "do you want me to have sex with her?"

"I want you to have some fun, kid! Jesus! I mean, the hell with it," and he gave me the finger and such.

I sensed my caution was going to screw everything up. "Okay! Look—what do I say to her?"

"You just take her in the back, tell her, and do it."

"Uh-huh." And I got a real strong rush, something like stroking a down-the-line double at Lincoln Mall Video Baseball. I mumbled, "Just take care of Lottery Woman, no more than three tickets," and I think maybe I just kind of found myself walking towards the storage room. What *was* I thinking? *Free-living, experimentation,* crap like that. Leah was in there, too, in the mind, but I convinced myself that she'd approve of the experiment.

"Trisha, I want to show you something back here."

I usually wasn't that forward in talking to her, but she didn't look at me funny or anything. *She just expects people to be the way they are,* I thought.

"Okay."

We stepped into the storage room amongst boxes everywhere, scattered on the floor, and I said, "I was wondering, uh, you don't have to if you don't want to, but I was wondering if you'd have sex with me." Sounds bullshit, but that's what I said. And it seemed very wrong to say what I'd said.

She paused a second, then said, "Huh? With you?" She laughed. "Sex? You wanna fuck?"

She didn't seem disgusted, just surprised. I said, "I mean, I'll pay or whatever, and I'll be nice."

"I'm not a fucking whore!" Her damp curls and such took on life.

"Sludge Man said you were."

"You believe everything anybody tells you."

"No, I just . . . I'm sorry, I'm really sorry, I really like you."

I babbled some more while imagining blowing my and Sludge Man's brains out, but from out of nowhere she said, "Look, look, I'll do it, you know," and made to pat me, though missed. "You know, you're all right. . . . Look, I won't do it for free, but I'm happy to do it for just twenty bucks. But look," she grabbed my wrist, "I'm not a fucking whore!"

I wasn't about to argue. Twenty bucks, who's to say what's a whore? Plus, she'd said I was nice.

"Where are we going to do it?" she said, and smiled a crooked tooth, melting me. Both nice and sexy, a miracle.

"I don't know," I said. "We can't. . . . It'd be too loud in here."

"How about the freezer?" she offered, pointing to the walk-in fridge. "The freezer'll be fun." And she smiled again. Sweet Trisha, I thought in my jumble, she's Rhode Island like me. I can be all of me with her.

"Yeah, fun. That's the walk-in fridge, actually. But I don't know, you can still see."

"We can move the boxes around. Come on, it'll be fun." I was glad that it would be fun and not just dirty, as she led me by the belt buckle into the walk-in.

She seemed kind of happy, then. Christ, she'd said *I* was weird. She seemed happy to be doing it, she said, "This'll be good, this'll be good, come on, Dairy Mart Kid."

In the walk-in we stacked some milk crates up to the ceiling, and Trisha commented on how the cold air felt neat on her butt, and I agreed. I had the condom, and there we went, first standing, then on the floor. It was a slow rhythm and very exciting, once I got over my fear of sticking to the metal walls and floor. I could smell her sweat, and kind of a basic smeared body odor, and behind it all the mist of Camels, which made it all feel supremely nasty but therefore better for the nonce. I remember it being nice to close my eyes and plant my head between her shoulder and neck, tasting her sour, cold coating.

I felt kind of crappy afterwards, like I usually did afterwards with Leah or alone. I was also cold. I apologized to Trisha for not giving her pleasure, as far as I could tell.

"It was okay," she said. "You know. You're okay. I mean it's never *great*. It's never what it's supposed to be. The freezer was fun, huh?"

I let myself get a bit hazy, closed my eyes. "I've never been with a prostitute before," I murmured, sounding in retrospect like a rich brat on *Masterpiece Theatre* or somesuch.

"I'm not a fucking prostitute!"

I felt extra crappy then. She was still kind of sitting on me and putting my leg to sleep; when I opened my eyes, I must admit I was a bit annoyed by the fact that she was swigging a Papaya Punch and looking just to the side of me with an aggressive, lowered-eyes Cranston pout that I knew quite well from the mall.

Then the ceiling beeper went off, indicating that someone had entered the store. I eventually focused enough to look out from behind the milk crates, and, peering above the butters but underneath the juices, and through the glass, I saw Lottery Woman. Sludge Man was feeding her tickets, rolls of ten at a time.

"Oh, my God," I said, envisioning Lottery Woman's weekly welfare money in Sludge Man's pocket. "I can't believe I left him in charge."

"I'm not a fucking whore. You know, it's really shitty of you not to listen to me."

I looked at her and she was Trisha from Cranston, sneering, vanishing eye corners. It had been ridiculous to think she'd ever really *be* for me, or me for her. I finally said something that I completely meant. "I'm a piece of shit. You're right. I'm sorry." So I gave her a bunch of money from my pants. I'd forgotten to palm the till. She squeaked a bit as she got up to get dressed.

When we emerged into the brightness of the main part of my Dairy Mart Kingdom, scraggly Lottery Woman was staring at me. She was a sad, sad woman.

"Hi!" I said, hoping to make her happy.

She looked at me and left.

Sludge Man was gone.

I went behind the counter and all of the lottery tickets were gone. He hadn't taken any money from the register, but he'd pocketed the lottery money. Weird. His own weird morality.

Then I heard Trisha leaving with a mumble.

I wondered if I was supposed to see some connection between Trisha and Sludge Man. If Rhode Island was out to get me. I sat on a crate behind the counter, itchy, neglecting my cleaning duties for a while.

***

But a couple of hours later, it was Friday morning sunshine, and I was handling the rush with skill and ease. Sticky underwear, but proud of my Kingdom. Explaining the lottery money was going to be a challenge, but I'd figure something out. I'd figure it out in my Kingdom. And a tingle was beginning to creep back in, just a hint, but building—*maybe it'll happen with Trisha again. Even though I know it's meaningless, maybe I could just get excited by the excitement.* Because that's the way of it, you know: it builds up, it crashes into dust, then it builds up again, so just be happy about the build-ups, yes, yes. And be happy about Trisha, too.

Then Jeannie walked in, red-eyed, with downturned mouth and such, poking into stuff and saying there was a problem.

So I'll tell you what maybe happened. Jeannie maybe told me that Lottery Woman had called her in tears at 4 a.m., saying that she'd seen me coming out of the back room with a stain on my pants, and meanwhile she'd spent all her welfare money, seventy bucks, to some crazy person with a beard behind the counter. And she only had four winners, all a dollar each. And Jeannie maybe said it was sad, I was a good worker, but maybe I had to go. She was very disappointed, having expected better from a Brown student.

And maybe I never saw any of them again, and Leah busted up with me that weekend in New York, admitting with great dramatic flair that she'd been sleeping with some alternative type for weeks. Maybe I took it okay, but didn't tell her about Trisha. And the next summer I qualified for a fellowship to Germany and never looked back, and never had to work in a Dairy Mart again.

But none of that means shit. What I think about, when I get lonely, is standing there in that sunshine moment before Jeannie came in, standing sticky, and thinking I'd see Trisha again.

Dolphin

I work up near the Falls, eight-to-five with an hour for lunch. For a couple years, on Tuesdays and Thursdays, I used that hour to go see the dolphins at the aquarium.

My keyboard keys at work had the same soft give as the buttons on the aquarium vending machine. G8, the Snickers thunked down, 323.6 for edema, another G8 for another Snickers, License #62 that's Nurse Barnett, B4 and the *schwat* of the pretzels, I never felt so nimble, nor so capable, nor so whole, as I did on those mornings leading up to my aquarium visits.

At the aquarium I'd take my food upstairs to the circular railing and look down into the pool below. Three fat dolphins swam endless circles. Dolphins are allowed to be fat, because they manage to be graceful as well, so people forgive the fat.

During the show they leapt high and nosed rubber balls. The ensuing splashes didn't quite reach the spectator deck.

***

At some point during my aquarium years, I took a class at ECC. I dropped out after a month but did manage to read a few articles in the library by some New Age Nut from California named Loomis. Some of that New Age stuff reached into me, back then. This Loomis guy wrote that penning up dolphins was like penning up God, and that paying admission to aquariums was like *enabling the Dark Force.* I thought, yeah, yeah, but I live in Buffalo, how else can I see dolphins? In California they probably swim up to your front door. But still I felt a little guilty for going to the aquarium.

I wrote these thoughts to the teacher as my "journal response." I'm embarrassed to admit that I remember the exact words of her reaction, indeed I can *see* the words. Her handwriting was very precise, as was her angular face. She wrote in purple pen in the margin: *Interesting—but I don't think Loomis was making a moral judgment.*

I felt guilty anyway. I wanted to tell the dolphins that I appreciated their being what they were, fat and alive, and that I was sorry they were penned. I figured if I told them that, the guilt would go away.

But I didn't know how to talk to them. The trainers claimed to be able to talk to them: two short whistles meant *dinnertime*, three long ones meant *ball*, stuff like that. Loomis said that was nothing, that you could *really* communicate with dolphins if you stared at their eyes and put all of your various life energies into the stare. *Try to send just one or two messages*, he wrote. *Like, "Your eyes are the jewels of the sea."* That sounded like a wasted message to me; I would have said, *I'm sorry you're penned, I love you.* But at any rate, if you followed his directions, the dolphins would know generally what you meant, and they might send you something in return, if they were in the right mood. *But your eyes must be no more than a foot from theirs.*

From where I stood at the aquarium, maybe a hundred feet away, their eyes were tiny black hyphens. The staff wouldn't let you get any closer. I called down to Marnie, a trainer with a huge, perfectly tied hair knot, and asked her if I could come down to the trainers' deck. "Oh, God, no," she said. "You're not a trainer, the dolphins would be frightened." She paused as she knelt to do something mysterious with a hose. Then, still fiddling with the hose, she said, "It's too bad the spectator deck is so high up. It doesn't have to be *that* high, you know. But that's the way they built it, and the only alternative is to bring you folks down here, and that's no good." She knew lots of stuff, did Marnie. She never asked me to hang out with her or anything, though.

Yeah, I could have broken in at night and visited the dolphins, gripped their faces and looked into their eyes—but someone would have caught me, hauled me away, called *me* a nut. But not a rich California nut. Just a data-enterer in Buffalo—send her to County General, or county jail. Loomis, now, he owned twenty miles of California beach, no one was hauling him anywhere. He said he'd made a mint in Internet stocks, and that there was nothing wrong with that.

***

The aquarium workers must have thought I was screwed up and maybe I was, I mean I did go in there a lot, instead of doing lunch with friends, going out for drinks, working out, snorting lines, whatever it was they did.

One day, a few minutes before the show, Marnie called up to me from the deck. "You love dolphins so much, Jennifer. You should have been a marine biologist."

"Yeah," I said, "I know, I know, but . . . it's hard to make a switch. When you've started a career, you know." Besides, I thought. I was never any good in science. *Marine biologist*, with all those complicated underwater computers and whatnot, Lord, she must have been kidding. I don't even know how to invest in Internet stocks.

That day about seven of us were leaning on the railings looking down. The usual type of crowd. A Bills Jacket. A couple parents with whining kids. The fathers always had beards and didn't want to be there. That day a father pointed to the dolphins and said to his son, "Them's good eatin'!" The kid and the father laughed and snorted. They bonded.

On the floor near me were a bunch of uneaten Milk Duds. Some kid had dropped her Milk Duds. I wondered if her parents had bought her more. F5 in the machine. I kept looking at the squashed Milk Duds.

The show had already started when I looked up. I tried to focus all my energy on staring at the dolphins, like Loomis had suggested, even though I was too far away for it to do any good. I wanted to cleanse my mind of the Milk Duds and the bonding and other accumulated crud. I tried to believe that the dolphins, even though I couldn't talk to them, could make me feel better, by showing me how to be simultaneously fat and graceful.

The whistling dolphin was doing so, and they were all about to demonstrate echolocation, when a speck appeared in my eye. It looked like an enormously fat dolphin was jumping in from the railing. Then *schwack* it hit the water, and a beautiful, huge, blue-white teacup of water formed in front of all our eyes, not just mine, with little tinkles spilling out the sides. A few drifted onto my face, and for a second my whole body electrified, and I realized I felt *exactly* like I had when the cops finally came and cuffed and carted my asshole father away, *out* of my life, never let him back, *yes* yes, a changed life. I knew right away it was the same feeling, thanks dolphin.

But then when the huge dolphin surfaced, it wasn't a dolphin. It was a person. The Bills jacket guy. He'd jumped in. Someone was screaming. I told myself to look at the dolphins, find their eyes, but for a long second I couldn't stop staring at Bills Jacket's head. His bald spot was glowing, he was smiling, and a gleaming black seemed to shoot out from his eyes. Then I looked to the dolphins, and they'd gathered in under the deck.

Bills Jacket shouted, "Hey, dolphin, hey?" and one dolphin started gliding over to him, like a soft bullet. Then the pool exploded. Four people crashed in from the trainers' deck, and everything became a mass of flailing humans and foam. I couldn't see any dolphins under all of that. Then someone turned the lights off, and I felt a sugar-sick from the Snickers and got the hell out of there.

Afterwards at my terminal, I wondered about the dolphins. They'd bolted when Bills Jacket had jumped in; they'd seemed terrified. Maybe dolphins don't want to be near us, I thought, maybe they don't even like Marnie and Loomis. Maybe you can only get near them if you train them, if you hold back their food until they jump up and nose balls for you. How perverse is that? The whole thing's perverse, never go back. Stop thinking about dolphins, find something else to think about.

But I couldn't stop, because of that lone bullet dolphin at the last second swimming over toward Bills Jacket. Maybe the dolphins had balked at first not out of fear, but just because their routine was broken. And maybe the bullet dolphin was swimming over to Bills Jacket so as to check things out. Take him for a ride back to the others. Communicate. Maybe, maybe not. I don't know. But maybe.

The dolphin pool was closed for about a month. When they opened back up, they'd built a Plexiglass shield up to the ceiling—no way to get into that pool ever again. I didn't go to the aquarium much after that.

***

I heard two women in the office a couple months back talking about dolphin swimming pools at Club Med or wherever they were going. Margaritas and dolphins. And I think I've heard whispers or dreams about California, that out there in LoomisLand are places where if you pay a lot, you get to swim with the dolphins. I don't know. I don't know. Maybe I'll get out there someday. I doubt I could afford whatever it costs to swim with dolphins. And I still don't know if they'd even like it.

Peretuck, Early Seventies

Something went wrong somewhere. I've been living in this town my whole life and every year I feel more cut-off, but I don't leave. And I'm thinking a lot lately that maybe Mary Lawson was what went wrong.

I was, I don't know, a pretty lonely-but-normal kid. Teenaged. I went to Peretuck Catholic High School, it's this horrible, horrible, old, brickish, shit-brown shut-it-down type of thing, it was old even then. And you just did what you did, most of us Catholics still lived by the river then, just fifteen, eighteen, well Christ, twenty-five years ago. Now it's all . . . the same, everybody lives everywhere, and I don't think I like it that way. I think Catholics should live by the river, and the rest of the people should live in the rest of the town and go to the rest of the schools, but that's just not the way it is.

There were I think fifty-two of us in my class. So I played football, nobody gave half a shit really, it was a basketball school at heart, and we were terrible in football. But of course we had our one Big Game on Thanksgiving, and they came out of the woodwork to see that one. We played Jesuit High from fifteen miles down the road and got the living crap kicked out of us every year. The fans, the parents, the bottles, the cowbells, they'd all be gone by the middle of the third quarter. The game and the season would both wind down in their special ass-freezing 42-6 way, and sophomore and junior years Coach Dwyer threw me and the other scrubs in there in the fourth quarter to die, only goddamn time we'd get all year really and we're out there against these monsters in red, just don't run my way, oh fuck, and I'm taken out by a muck-covered pulling guard, twelve yard gain, icy pain. And afterwards? Blurred, forget these cute stories about the dance and the rosy-cheeked cheerleaders, none of that, instead my buddy D'Addario and I tramped home and fired the ball around Daley Textile parking lot in the dark, the wind snappling windowpanes. But I liked some of it, you know, I wouldn't mind whipping parking-lot square-outs to D'Addario right now. But he got a job a few years back in Arizona, I think, one of those states out there.

When I was a senior, I met Mary Lawson. She was from our sister school Saint Anne's and was Irish as Irish is, yeah red hair and forever pudgy cheeks Mary Lawson Mary Lawson say it thirty times make a thousand rhymes. She took my hand on ratty couch in third-story ricket apartment, her father off at the track, her Mom in bed with the crosses and the TV set, Mary took my hand and said, slow and whiny and ruminative, "What do you think of that? Huh, Terry? I told Sister that Jesus wouldn't have done that if he was following the same rules he'd set down in the other place."

"Yeah. Hr-hm. Well, you know, I think uh . . . Jesus is pretty confusing but uh . . . what he did in general I think was okay."

"Exactly!" And she pulsed a little. "That's what I'm telling her, you have to look at the whole picture. Sister didn't get it." Mary put her other hand on my hand, she bounced the whole hand sandwich on my knee. "You know I like to talk to you, Terry."

"Yeah, it's, you know, somewhat of a mutual situation," I mumbled and stumbled, didn't want to be too girly precious, but Jesus Mary if I could have told you then I would have told you then, about sitting there like that, the crack you made inside me, the flipperflops and candymelt ooze, down near Daley Textile we skipped two o'clock flatrocks, when cuteyblue jacket wrapped my head 'round your lint-sweatered breasts and we giggled and moaned in the leathery early-morning purple-watered battery acid factory mishmash dump all I wanted was your stomach Mary, and a kiss on the neck and a whisper in the dark, "I love you, Terry, I love you," and Peretuck seemed okay.

She hated my football and so I skipped most practices to talk and lie and scrabble around with her. Coach Dwyer rumbled and lapped me but wouldn't cut me, as we only had twenty guys on the team. A week before Thanksgiving Mary and I sat on her living-room floor after dinner trying to do math homework while her plate-clattering little brother flew around the apartment.

"You're gonna score a touchdown for Mary, hey Terry?"

"No, uh . . . I don't think so, kid, I only play defense, you know, and uh . . . not too often at that."

"Doug, Dougie Packard's brother Stevie plays both ways, off, offense, defense, the whole thing!"

"Yeah, well, Steve Packard's an ass—" Mary shot me a warning look, dull green eyes glinting anger in the room dark. "Stevie's a good ballplayer," I corrected, "but I kind of suck—"

She whacked me on the ear. Mary was gentle but knew how to hit. "Watch your language!"

"Sorry," I woozied out, and lay back for a minute. She held my hand and sat there like an Indian, long green wool skirt spread out like a picnic table in front of her.

"It's okay. Just be nice."

She scratched my shag of hair and I disappeared into her. "Mary Mary, you've got to come to my game on Thursday, please."

"I hate it. It's horrible."

"I know, kid, but I'm gonna be all alone, everybody's gonna leave at halftime and I'm gonna freeze to death we'll lose by 50 points and Dwyer'll throw me out there in the second half, they'll pound me into dust—"

"Why don't you just quit? It's ridiculous!"

"Well . . . I've only got the one game left, you know. . . ."

"But you hate it! It's—forget it, I don't want to talk about it, just hold my hand." I did what she said because she was Mary, brooding, lip-chewing Mary staring holes in the carpet, staring Jesus holes and heaven and love while she twiddled my thumbs with hers and I murmured groggily by her lap, "Awww, la-la-la-la. . . ."

She came to the game.

We were 1 and 6, that's one win six losses, Jesuit was only 3 and 4, the game meant nothing to nobody but Mary was there in dirty white rainyday rubbercoat, up in the corner of their little one-sideline grandstand all alone she didn't move, didn't wave, just sat there shrouded like death, and I could hardly see her as the mist thickened and the snow started down, guilt like a clamp.

The game sucked, flat-out, nobody could do anything but run two-yard plows because of the snow and the goddamn skin-cracking *cold*, it wasn't even remotely glorious, just boring, on the sideline I prayed for it to end as my whole body chiggered except for the toes, frozen banana popsicles, D'Addario and I got in twice for the kickoffs and couldn't even see the ball, just jogged down on our heels, "Show some hustle!" Coach Dwyer growled, "Fuck you!" D'Addario spat back brilliantly, I just tried to survive and search for Mary, she sat motionless, accusing, a gray smudge in the duskish murk. And I remember thinking in my clear-minded revelatory eighteen-year-old way, "What a supreme asshole the male species is, what supreme stupidity!"

Twenty seconds left, we're losing six-nothing, maybe thirty people left watching, Mary frozen like a statue in the distant gloom, and I'm standing near the bench trying to calculate exactly how long it will be until Warmth when smash! massive sickening collision, red shirts in front of me, on top of me, I look up and there goes Little Johnny Lambo, tiny sophomore who wasn't even a half-bad kid, he's spinning like a demon top down the sidelines *free*, I'm on the ground wondering if he's even going the right way but he's in the end zone on his knees *we tied the game*! I actually cared, I actually ran down there and pounded his too-big head, numbers were swirling all around me, "Twenty-two, twenty-two," we hadn't beaten them in twenty-two years, or since 1922, we'd *never* beaten these Jesuit bastards, they'd murdered our fathers, enslaved our children, and now all we had to do was trot Packard out there to kick the extra point, glee, glee, but here's confusion, guys running back and forth I can't see but now I hear Dwyer and it's "two, two," the moron wanted us to run it in for two points it made *no sense*, all Packard had to do—tall, blond, snotty but straight-on Packard—all he had to do was kick it through but Dwyer's got them out there lining up for two and I lost it, couldn't even feel myself, I ran right up helmet off, "What the hell are you doing, Dwyer?" "We're going for two, shut up," and I screamed every word I could think of, "You fucking stupid ugly bastard what the hell are you trying to pull you suck like the puke-ass school—" And he cracked me down, hard, I've often thought I could have sued him, not for hitting me but for that call, heinous it was (and he never has explained it), they fumbled the try, it ended 6-6, D'Addario dragged me off, half-conscious and I'd barely played, in the wooden shack of a locker room I came to and found a yellow stain on my crotch.

But Christ, Mary took care of me that night. I thought she'd hate me but she just put her arm around me in her *bedroom*, the door locked, I cried and cried, "I don't know what *happened* out there, Dwyer smacked me and there was cold everywhere and we should have won the goddamn game—"

Mary enveloped me, so huge all around me, "Shh. Shut up. No, little fool, just, no, just shut up because it doesn't matter, it doesn't matter, none of that matters and you know it, you're all that counts, just be quiet and later you can tell me about my hair, you can tell me about what we're gonna do in the spring, and afterwards, oh Terry Terry Terry you're my little fool, my little fool who I met in school," she sang me a ridiculous little sweetie-pie song, I snuffled and warbled and felt my wetness on her sweater.

***

End of that senior year Mary got a scholarship to a college in the city, two hundred miles away, I just went to the state school upriver a bit, but things were okay for a while. I just read and read and read, didn't go to class that much but read all the books, and Mary and I sent five letters a week. She loved me desperately, she wrote, and I believed her, the letters got wild and bit like little rabbits, she wanted to get married right then, that minute, she'd never sounded so crazed before but what the hell, she loved me. Christmas time we merged in Peretuck, we went down behind the factory, we played with her little brother in those frozen, joyous, no-school afternoons, we put the tree up all ragged but spangled. Everything was holy. I went back to school and it was Mary Mary Mary and then . . . something went wrong, and Cripes I'm telling this epic boring story of my life because something went wrong but I still can't fingerpoint exactly what it was, when the hell or why the hell it happened down there, but something went wrong.

Her letters drifted off, vaguish, all on a sudden. I called her from my beer-drenched hallway hell and she's inaudible and reedy, "I love you, Terry, I love you, I have to go, though." I was supposed to make a voyage to her in the spring, St. Patrick's Day weekend, and I started to headache and sweat about it, of course I thought "another guy," but it really shouldn't have been possible, you must see this, Mary and I came together like a puzzle, like pancakes and butter, two cats curled up, something like that *should—not—end.*

I got there whitefaced off the train, she took me to her room and there's five other people there, three guys and two girls slopped around and horrible arrogant acrid smoke, "Uh, yeah, hi, nice to meet you, I'm Terry, uh. . . ." The girls had beads in their hair and crap on their eyes, but the guys, oh Christ, this is '71 or '72 and I know I've got to be accepting and I've tried to mind-expand through books before and since, but the guys had earrings, I just, *earrings*, it was too much for me, I guess I was, is, I'm a goddamn Peretuck boy at heart.

"Hey, do you indulge?" and one of the guys, he had a bandanna and a beard, he passed me some fungus-looking thing, I fled to the bathroom and cornered Mary.

"What the hell is this, I thought you had one roommate!"

"I do, shh, shh, will you? Angela has a lot of friends, and they're my friends, too. Just be nice."

"You didn't tell me about all this! I don't understand . . . how this could happen so damn *sudden*, I mean, what is this shit, why are you with these people, who are these guys—"

I'd never talked to her like that, it was like finding out my mother was a whore and then stabbing her, stabbing her.

"I didn't tell you because I knew you'd be like this. After—ahhh! After Christmas, being back home, when I got back here, I—agh!—I need to grow, Terry!"

"Well . . . *grow*, I mean, I don't know what the hell you're talking about, but I just thought we could get some kind of a privacy situation going here, you know, I mean . . . you're the one who sent me all this stuff about getting married. . . ."

"I know, and I'm sorry about that."

"Well, what the hell is going on? I mean . . . shit! You don't . . . want to marry me, ohh. . . ."

"I don't know! I don't know what's going on, but Terry, there's other people in the world—"

"Yeah no shit there's other people in the world, you goddamn—"

"Don't talk to me like that."

"Sorry." To me she was still Mary of course, she'll always be for me, but she was lost under some layer, or maybe I was the one who was lost, but anyway I was gone the next night after a vision of her with a needle near her foot and a chilled smile on her lips, Mr. Bandanna sucking on her bare middle, and Mary moaning, "Come on, join the fun, Terry, it'll be okay, join the world," her lips purple, sunglasses on her face, her red hair dyed blonde, her red hair dyed blonde, her red hair dyed blonde.

***

I remember a few months after that, it was summertime suppertime, dust dancing in the lightshaft as me and my family ate beans, and it was weird because the TV was busted. Everything was quiet for the first time in history. Someone had to talk but no one made the move. Finally Mom said from out of nowhere, "Have you heard from Mary at all?"

The beans tasted like cotton all of a sudden. "Ungh . . . no."

"Well, she was a sweet girl. You should call her up, just as a friend."

"Mmm. No. She's, uh, she's not even around. D'Addario heard she's living in the city with some guy for the summer. She's real—she's into that city thing."

"Well you know, Terry . . . maybe you have to be more like that. I'm not saying you should be a . . . *hippie* or anything, but maybe you should be a little more modern. I mean you dress just like your father did twenty-five years ago. And his father before that, really. . . ."

"Uh-huh. Yeah. Well you know, Ma, maybe I should wear an earring. I remember these guys down in—"

"No son of mine will ever wear an earring. I'd fucking ... cut his ear off."

That was the longest speech Dad ever made at the table. No lie. I shut up.

Marjorie

Earlier tonight, I had a revelation.

I was sitting on a barstool, drinking decaf, in the downstairs of my mother's condo. *Jeopardy* was on.

Upstairs, Ma started moaning. Not too loudly, though. She sounded maybe still asleep, dreaming about Hell or something. I sipped.

Then, "Marjorie, Marjorie, Marjorie." A miserable bleat now, the way she almost always sounds now.

"What?" I yelled. One of *Jeopardy*'s categories was "Classical Music." Maybe I could get one right. Or at least relearn something.

"Marjorie!" As if the world depended on it.

The bearded brilliant from Yale picked "Madonna" for four hundred. I threw my coffee on Ma's cherished white carpet and pounded upstairs.

Her bedroom has smelled the same for two years now. Like the lion cage down at the Providence Zoo. Rotting meat. Feeding on her own flesh and sweat.

Through a fog I could see that her catheter had slipped out. Maybe. All I knew was it didn't look the way the nurses had said it should look. The bag was hanging off the side of the bed. Urine turns brown when staining a faded white sheet.

Ma's dying, can't take care of me or her no more. Hair all gone from head, but now peeking out above lips. My Ma.

"Marjorie Marjorie. Mah-jorie. Put it. Put it back in."

"No, Ma," I began to whine. Little Girl Me. Go hug Ma for comfies. But she was lying in piss and stink and all she ever does these days is complain.

"Marjorie. Put it in."

I wasn't going to put the catheter back in. I'm not a goddamn nurse. My degree's in music, for God's sake. And she hates the damn thing anyway.

I left the condo through the sliding doors, because she wouldn't be able to hear me leave that way. On the car radio I could find only "classic hits," music that sounds meaningful at first, but then you think about it, and you realize it means less than nothing.

And then I had my revelation. Even as part of me screamed to go back in and nestle on Ma's breasts and take care of her, all at once my revelation in this particular world was that I was not going to be saved. I was a selfish pig: letting my mother die, doing nothing with my life. I didn't know if there were a God or a heaven, but in any case, I wasn't going to either one.

My immediate reaction to my revelation was, "Well, the hell with it then. I won't worry about anything until I'm ready to die." And so I came to this motel and snagged a room and bought some candy and Coke and blasted the air conditioner. I'm still about two hundred below the limit on this Visa, no reason to worry right now.

In maybe an hour or so, when this room starts to close in on me, I'll ponder the implications of an unsavable life, wherein my passage on Earth is the best passage I can ever hope for, and the wind will phoosh out of my throat, and I'll worry about Ma, sick in the condo, and I'll ponder how embarrassing it is that I'm living back in Passaket with my mother a year and a half after graduating college, and I'm jobless, and forty thousand B.U. bucks in debt, way worse off than all those drunken, racist Passaket jocks and jockettes and rapers and snorters that I always hated and prayed to get away from back in high school, the ones I rejoiced to escape upon leaving for B.U., the ones I thought I'd transcended,

yes to them I was snotty little Marjorie who wouldn't go to the parties and the games, who wouldn't watch the snuff flick that everyone whispered and snickered about the week before the junior prom, snotty bitch didn't know how to have fun, what the hell made her think she was above it all, wasn't good at sports, or straight A's, though she was pretty nice-looking,

you're pretty nice-lookin', said the hockey goalie, hoarse and beery in my ear the night I went to my cousin's to play her a piece I'd written but instead found her in the center of that weekend's big party because Aunt and Uncle were away, and oh look, pretty bitch Marjorie finally came to a party, and goalie got me in the corner, *you're so hot, you should come to more parties*, Passaket's version of a gentle compliment, and then he was burping in my ear, gentle goalie, horrid, but I let him proceed, all horrid,

yes I'll be worrying about these things soon and will decide to go home to Ma around midnight, but then I'll feel pissed about getting only three hours in the motel room for my fifty bucks, but Mother Dear's catheter will still be out and she'll still be groaning and agonized, and my throat will close completely and my stomach will cramp. I know all this will happen, it's happened before.

But right *now*, fresh from realizing I can't be saved, I feel... loose. Yeah! Floppy neck. Scratch my head with both hands. Okay to be lazy, relax. Let mind and fingers wander.

***

My fingers were on a Boston University piano the first time William saw me. I was practicing for my Intermediate Piano class, which I needed to pass in order to graduate. This was two years ago.

William said that my playing lit him up. "You really seem to work at it," he told me. "It's moving."

No drunken Passaket goalie or crack dealer had ever said anything like that to me. And now here was this Ph.D.-seeker from South Carolina saying he found me, or my playing, "moving." "Slightly surprising" probably would have been more accurate for him to say, as I was probably just the only B.U. undergraduate he'd ever seen who wasn't talking about last night's keg party, but who was instead making mash of a supposedly simple Bartók piece that made me cry when others played it. I wanted to be able to make someone else cry, but I couldn't get the piece down, I couldn't get the left-hand melody.

So William didn't cry, but he did say "moving," and I allowed that word to echo. So then I was in his bed, and he was on top of me, whispering, "I like the way your bangs spread out, I like the way they hang down when you play the piano," and I let it flatter and tingle me even though things like bangs are meaningless. He came too quickly so I didn't have a chance, but at least he held me afterwards instead of just going to the fridge to grab a brew like a Passaket asshole would. All around me were thousands of his books, some in other languages, a few about religion, stuff that really *should* mean something. And even though he then started smoking a joint, I let myself believe that it didn't annoy me, that he was so smart he must have a good reason to smoke it, that he'd teach me about the books, that life would become richer in various ways, that I'd get further away from Passaket in various ways.

After he'd sucked on the joint very seriously a couple of times, he said, "Yeah, that was really sweet, you really do work at things. The piano, this." He smiled and closed his eyes.

This reflection initially struck me as being ridiculous, but then I thought, *It's a brilliant poetic comparison from the English Ph.D.*, you know, sex compared to the piano, brilliant. And I was very pleased to apparently be doing both of them well. So I said, "Yeah, thanks," and giggled wickedly, and kissed him and then went down on him, and his beard tasted like pot and his cock kind of sour, but I thought about how it had just been inside another part of me and I tried to make it all mean something, in some brilliant way. And he was moaning, "Yeah, work it, work it, Marjorie."

***

I really *was* working at the piano, though. That was the problem with it. Five goddamn years of trying to get my bachelor's degree, of constructing a new plan for a new major every other month when the old one would collapse, finally settling back to music, which is where I'd started—and I still had to *work* at Intermediate Piano. I just couldn't merge two melodies at the same time. I simply wasn't good enough: no self-pity, just a fact.

Unfortunately I was realizing this just as William and I started getting together. I'd already decided that I would give up piano when the course was over, and I'd begun strumming three chords on a guitar instead, trying to simplify Ravel for the masses. Sometimes this undertaking made me feel significant, but more often just embarrassed and pretentious. I feared that William would become bored with me, but he said he wouldn't. So after we both finished at B.U., I tagged along after him out to Amherst. I figured I'd cling to him until he got bored.

I have dull blue eyes, the color of a popsicle after all its juice has been sucked out. William pointed out that when we made love, they'd shine. I usually wasn't able to let go of enough of myself to come, but at least he was gentle when he held me, and we didn't talk about my not coming.

One time afterwards he quoted Byron, *And all that's best of dark and bright meet in her aspect and her eyes*, and we both laughed because it was pretentious yet romantic, that whole cute combo.

But I was scared about something, and I thought the fear might be why I was still a little tight inside, so I said, "I wish you'd talk less about my eyes and hair and more about me being 'moving.'"

"What?"

"Just . . . you know, looks don't mean anything, really. Right?"

"Well, sure they do," he said, and for some reason his accent really struck me for the first time, the oddness of the vowels, blondish-red, like his beard. My voice sounded black aside his.

"It's silly to deny it," he went on. "But hey, if you don't want me to compliment you, I won't." He laughed briefly through his nose and took a drag of his joint.

I decided I was screwing things up for no good reason. Let him say nice things about my eyes and hair and don't worry about it. So I tossed my bangs in a stereotypically seductive way and said, "Never mind, sexy," and reached over and inhaled a bit because I knew that he preferred me to. You need to make compromises if you want a relationship to last.

***

Amherst was our *stepping stone to the future,* according to William. Furnished with his doctorate, he had secured a position teaching *Seinfeld* and Talking Heads to young women at Mount Holyoke College. I, on the other hand, was supposed to be figuring out *which degree to get next.* In the meantime I had the *perfect little in-between job*, shuffling papers for the music department. Jonathan, a young, ponytailed history professor with a glued-on half-grin, marveled that the combination of my boyfriend and employment situations enabled me to attend both faculty and staff parties, the sublime to the ridiculous, the best of both worlds, because the faculty parties had the best drinks and God only *knew* what went on at the staff parties. When I told Jonathan that I didn't go to parties, he pretty much stopped talking to me.

Two streets over from our apartment was Emily Dickinson's house, so I asked William to help me understand her poems, even though he preferred teaching Janet Jackson and all that stuff, which I never really got. But he was good about Dickinson, and I remember nice times in the bed, with the book propped on his knees and me holding him from behind and chinning his shoulder so I could see the poems. It was hard; you had to move words around, slip them into holes I couldn't see. This led to frustration and a pouting face for little Marjorie. But William said some poems were like that for him at the beginning, too. Eventually I got some of it. I felt sorry for the worm but pitied the bird as well.

William said, "Well, right, that's what it's about. So . . . good."

Once I got the words to fit, a few of the poems sang in my mind like no piano exercise ever had. *The Soul selects her own society*, I could dig that, it briefly validated me and consigned people like Jonathan to irrelevance. I mean, hell, by being a loner I was just imitating a successful person, a famous person. Famous Emily. And William said he didn't mind that I didn't hang with anyone but him.

So I took a couple of my guitar chords and set Dickinson to music, and stood under a birch in Lahey Park at lunchtime, with my fingers strumming, and my butt flexing, singing about the Soul selecting her own society. I didn't do Dickinson justice, but still I liked it.

And one time William said he liked it, too, that made me feel good, even though he'd had a couple of joints and was mellowly out-of-it at the time. I told him we were the Divine Majority, and he smiled and kissed me. The next morning, a Sunday in October, I dragged him out of bed and into the shower, and then out to the car and up a small Vermont mountain, the rest of the world watching football, reading the paper, buying Halloween candy, but we climbed up over cutesy town to the top, meadow-like with pecking virgin birds, and we drank our Gatorade, down just to sweatshirts, and held hands, and for once *I* felt like starting, out there above the smoke from cars and pot, and away from faculty and cokeheads and likewise, so I started to sway my hips and feel his middle hoping he would respond. And he did but was startled enough to not know what to say, so I sang my new song and led him in a stumble among idiot-twisted mountaintop trees, then pulled him down to our electric blanket lying in the grass, and his mouth and cock and everything tasted sweet and sober and clean and right, it was winter on top of that mountain and the wind sliced bullets into our pores, both of us freezing our butts off and laughing anyway, and maybe for once I came, or close to it anyway, I was up on top straddling him and looking down and singing, he was breathless and could only listen.

***

It was a couple weeks after that, around Halloween, that Ma got sick. She was screaming at William on the phone from Passaket, but I didn't have the guts to talk to her. "She says she's lying at the bottom of the stairs," he told me, holding his hand over the mouthpiece.

I tried to forget about it, but I kept imagining Ma there, unable to move, and thoughts flooded in that I knew were wrong but could not deny: boring imbecilic Passaket mother with her game shows and beer lying on her sacred white carpet, boring imbecile who used the life insurance from Dad not for a condo in Florida, where they'd know how to take care of her, or even in Smithfield, no, she decided to move two neighborhoods over to the "nice section" of Passaket, and now this, sloshing her way into my flawed-but-gentle Life with a Smart Person.

William and I sat down together in our combination kitchen/storage room that I had originally considered cute. Empty boxes everywhere, we were surrounded by cardboard Fragile mountains.

Not thrilled considering our financial situation but willing to help her out was William's mood. I remember thinking, *God this music is so sad*, on the classical station, moaning sounds in 5/4 time. They'd said the composer was from East Providence. Transcendence from a Rhode Islander. Why couldn't I nail transcendence with my music? What was wrong with me? And I remember wondering whether it was the Nutrasweet from my coffee that made me think sixteen things at once, and none of them steady, or was I just stupid like my mother?

William turned the radio off and said, "Well, look. There are essentially three choices. One, she can go into a nursing home, or some kind of assisted-living place." Scribbling it on his note pad, organized Professor William. "Two, you can get her a daytime health aide, um," scribble, "from what I can tell, her insurance covers part of either one of those, but you—or we, I guess—would have to help out somewhat. As I said before, I'm not thrilled with this situation, but you're her only child, and I'm willing to help a bit. And of course the third choice is for you to go take care of her, but . . . neither one of us wants that."

I was just thinking, *His beard is fuzzycute and tickly when he kisses my breasts, but now it's just a shield. Can't kiss him now.*

"What do you want to do, Marjorie."

"I don't know."

"Well." He quieted a moment.

I thought, *Well, here it is, what do smart people do when confronted with average people?* See, that's the risk, you can feel superior to your cute babe with her bangs and sometimes-sexy eyes, and get a nice kick out of all that, but she's a pain in the intellectual ass when push comes to shove.

But I was afraid to say any of that. Finally, he said, "Well, that's not good enough. What do you want to do?"

"I don't know! The day care thing sounds best, I don't know. I don't know." An oblivious window squirrel pecked at a nut.

"Day care? What do you mean?"

"Oh come on . . . smart guy." And then I squeezed up high on his thigh to show I was just kidding. "You know what I mean, the health aide thing, whatever."

But he wanted to stay serious. "What do you mean by 'smart guy'?"

"Oh come *on!*" I just wanted to change the channel; this show was boring. "Look—the health aide thing, let's do that."

"You realize that she'll still be alone much of the day that way—"

"Fine. Whatever. I don't know what to do. Let's go for a walk." I wanted to go strolling down Route 9 in my blue straw hat and make lonely people jealous of us.

"Marjorie, that's not good enough. I'm making a fair effort here, I think. She's *your* mother."

"Thanks for the info. I mean, come on—you're making me feel like one of your goddamn students."

He breathed in and held it, like he probably did with those same students. Except the really smart ones, what did he do with them? Then he said, "Look, Marjorie, at some point you have to make some decisions in your life. Right? It's fine to relax for a while, but it's probably time for you to start making decisions in your life. Right?"

"Huh?"

"Decisions! You have to make at least *some* decisions."

"About what?"

He heaved another breath, as if it was a big effort. "About your mother, and about your own life."

"What the hell are you talking about? Don't talk to me about my own life! Talk about my mother, but not *my* life."

"Why? You don't want to talk about skipping out of your job early and then going home to play the same four chords over and over?" He stared at me, his face pulling back while his arms stretched forward and his hands met on the table.

"Hey, I make money from my guitar," I flared, trying to sound tough, but wondering just how many more worms were going to squiggle out from under the rock he'd lifted.

"I see, so you want to talk about ten dollars one night a week from passing the hat at the coffeehouse? Is that what you want to talk about? Please."

I tried to say something clever like "It pays for a few of your joints" but it didn't come out right, just "Pays a few—fuck!" Then I was crying, and he was apologizing, but I still cried. I'd known this would happen, but it hurt anyway. God had set me up and then left me, a dead sapling deserted by the birds. Okay, it's crap compared to Dickinson, but as good as I can do. I don't claim to do better.

That was about the biggest argument we ever had—afterwards he had a way of avoiding them, of coming to bed when we had only enough energy for sex, of stretching out innocuous breakfast discussions about the window planter and bird feeder—but, inevitably, things got worse anyway.

He set up the health aide, even spent a day on the phone hammering out the insurance. I don't know why he did those things. I don't know why I did zilch. Ma was furious: "You're disgusting, you don't care about family. You should be here taking care of me, after all I've done for you," etcetera, after a while I'd just hang up.

And over and over, the same trite words in my head: *If I go to her, I'll be back in mindless Passaket, if I don't, I'll feel guilty,* blah blah, I hate my boring words, I can't make them sing.

The only time I felt halfway worthy was playing Monday night open mike at the coffeehouse. Okay, okay, it was no big deal, William. Fifteen people, clinking glasses, and a lot of *ha-ha*'s for some jokes I couldn't hear. Sometimes a couple in the front would listen, though, and that was all I wanted. No more than that, I swear.

One Monday in November they were having a famous alumna, Maria Trottier, back for a gala homecoming. She had a band and a video on VH-1. The video was a remake of "Big Girls Don't Cry," in which she danced around in bikini pajamas. When I wondered what the big deal was about this silliness, William explained to me that it was a brilliant "sort of post-post-feminist thing. The vamping bit. She's a sharp gal." So the place was jammed, and even William was there on the side, sitting with a couple of colleagues.

My three songs went okay. I skipped the middle verse of the Dickinson song by mistake, but of course no one knew. I finished with "Deportees," and though I wasn't really with the words due to my nerves, the crowd gave a lot of whoops because that song can't lose in Amherst, it's left-wing. Everyone was focused; for once they were there to listen.

But then Trottier came out, and they were pulling me back up on the damn stage because of some tradition that one of the amateur losers gets her moment in the sun with the returning hero. So I was standing there with my horrendous used guitar, uncut strings, while she was mumbling to me all these songs I'd never heard of. "How about 'Leg Room,'" I think she said, "or 'Urum Bu-bum.'" I think, looking back, that they were probably *her* songs, and of course I should have studied up ahead of time. But at the time all I could say was, "Uh, no, I don't know it, no, don't know that one either, look why don't you just play it, just let me get out of here," and her seemingly effortlessly nuanced harmonica-playing Other, with Inevitable Tattered-but-Perfectly-Arranged handkerchief around neck, so this absolutely Authentic partner-Other was saying snappily and scarily, "Come on, come *on*, let's just *do* it," and finally Trottier said, "'Wagoner's Lad,'" and I said, "Yeah! I know it," easy old folkie tune, and I tensed to play. I glanced at William, and he was smiling at me, first time in a while.

But then Trottier started tuning and I couldn't figure out what the hell she was tuning to. It sounded terrible, totally out of whack. I thought for a second that maybe she was just bad, but then I remembered who she was. Then she strummed an intro and began to sing and I was in another dimension, some shifted warp. She was singing the right words but playing some chords that didn't even exist, up around the eight and ninth frets.

I was afraid to say anything since she'd already started, so through the first two verses I just stood there with my hands frozen on my A-minor strings, poised for nothing. I couldn't even sing, because I couldn't figure out the key. Trottier looked at me once in the middle of a rounded nod, and then she looked away. To be forever stuck a chord-and-a-half below where you're supposed to be. I looked out at the faces for a place to flee, and William was staring at the wall, and I could hear a couple of people laughing, and I yearned to escape to the tiny, dingy bathroom next to the bar. I wanted to shrink and then hide behind a toilet for the rest of my life. Harmonica Dude took a solo and I finally leaned towards Trottier and said, "What the hell are you tuned to?" and she didn't even look up, just mouthed something like "Open D." And I'm sorry, life, William, I'm sorry I am who I am and I screw up when I do, but screw you too, because I've never heard of Open D, five years of college and they never taught me.

Someone, meaning well I suppose, said to me on the way out, "Better luck next time," and those four words hung in the air as William and I walked silently home. Suddenly I remembered walking these same Amherst streets many years before, lost, with Dad, at night, when I was a kid. Dad was drunk from the URI-UMass football game he'd dragged me to, and he couldn't find our car. When we finally got back to Passaket that night, Ma was watching the end of *The Sound of Music* on TV, and she remarked while staring at the final scene that she had been looking forward to watching the movie with me.

I told William none of this. All I said, while passing Dickinson's house, was, "Jesus, easy for her, easy for her. Easy for her to write and create. Goddamn lawyer father. Rich bitch, all that free time. She could afford to lock herself into her bedroom."

"Marjorie, don't talk about things you don't know," he said, his grip tightening as it jerked my arm. I'd never felt such a grip from him, and I thought I could feel my blood flow stopping. "I don't try to explain . . . music, so don't you try Dickinson."

"I'm just saying, she had it easy," I squeaked. "Am I wrong on that?"

"Oh, don't blame other people, Marjorie."

"For what?"

"Don't blame other people."

***

Right. But the thing is: I've grown to dislike most people in this world. Passaketers, academics, all the rest with their parties and drugs. I hate being near them. I didn't ask to be this way. Who's to blame for this state of affairs? Me me me, but still. Who made me so I should feel this way, different from how I'm supposed to be?

Other people make me tense. When I explain this to people, they say, "Oh, come on, Marjorie, stop whining and just be yourself." But that's bullshit. If I'm myself, it's almost always a disaster. Myself is the voices inside me. Those voices don't cut it at the Passaket keg party, or the faculty cocktail party. Or in the dining hall.

I had begun eating lunch by myself in that dining hall, reading, near these exotic decorative birds that were kept in a cage in the corner. I felt thousands of serpent eyes upon me, but I tried to focus on the reading. Sometimes I'd wish that William could be with me, so we could try to work things out, but he always had a class when I was free.

Then Jonathan, the professor who'd been fascinated by my peculiar faculty-staff dynamic, got bothered. He'd walk by and see me eating alone and say, "Are you being antisocial or do you really want to read?" Or, "John Steinbeck, huh?" His tones sounded cocky, but tones are tricky. You've got to let him benefit from the doubt. I mean, I think I was supposed to laugh, with the understanding that I knew Steinbeck was for kids and that I must be reading him for sociocultural reasons. I usually said, "I like to read," but every time I said this, Jonathan was already turning away and saying something just on the coffee-cup brim of intelligibility, like, "Okay, but blah buh another blah deception." And the day after my coffeehouse disaster, at Jonathan's moment of turning away, I looked down and some Steinbeck grandfather was saying, *You wouldn't worry so much about what other people think of you if you knew how seldom they did.* And Grandfather was full of shit, they were all full of shit.

I stood up and shouted, "Hey!" Jonathan turned half-around.

I really should have hit him; in retrospect, I can think of no argument against doing so. But at the time, as I raised the chair and focused on his lovingly crafted intellectual ponytail, something made me turn away. I wonder what it was.

At least it felt good when I smashed the table. Solid. So I wheeled and hit another empty table, and some of the chair broke, but I kept on smashing, my back to the squeals and shouts. Then I grabbed a stool and swung blindly, and whatever I hit sent a shudder up the stool, like the bat from when Dad forced me to try softball. Yelling, "Hey, Jonathan! Hey, everybody, hey, *everybody*!" Thinking, *Am I going nuts? Am I going nuts? Go nuts! Go nuts!*

The birds were going nuts, yabbering and flinging themselves against their cages, but I found myself suddenly standing still, center of attention and starting to shiver. I can't make anything last.

***

Not even beliefs. Like this one: I believe that if I look at a book, and some guy says I should look somewhere else, then it's his responsibility to deal with it. The questions are his. Got nothing to do with me. I want to keep believing that, but I can't.

The last time I saw William was a few weeks after my table assault. He kissed me on the lips goodbye. We'd lasted about a year.

The last evidence I had of his existence was in a hip new journal given prominent placement in the bookstore down in Providence. He published an article in there about Madonna. She's more than an artist, he wrote, she's a force of nature. She changes the way everyone thinks and lives and breathes and genders. And then he quoted some of her words, about how we can all find beauty if we all just get out there on the dance floor together and shake it, hard.

He even wrote, *You go, girl!* It's funny, but I've never figured out quite what the fuck that means.

When I think about the things I've done, I don't see the woman I want to be or should be. I wonder if people like William think about the things they do, or if they just do what they're good at. I wonder what's the difference between people like Doctor William, with his *Seinfeld* and Madonna and high-grade pot, and people like Moron Mother, with her *Home Improvement* and Frank Sinatra and Schlitz. I wonder why I can't flush either type out of my mind.

***

Lying in this trucker motel tonight after leaving Ma and realizing I can't be saved, I pretend for a while that whatever

I do is right. In this room with bed, coffeemaker, and TV. Vending machine right outside. All I need, and me. I hope this night never ends.

Later. Still. Later still I rub a pillow all over me and then burrow into it like a hamster. A just-right odor, combination of discharges. Licking my womanness. The pillow smiles on top of me. I want to look in the mirror and cut off all my hair and smile.

Touch my forehead with wet finger. Train my thoughts to some other place, no, to this here place. Swollen finger pulsing there. Jerk my legs like broken scissors. When I'm about to come, I tell the pillow. "I'm coming. Smile at me." And it really lasts.

And now this humming stillness. Like all of Rhode Island's seagulls inside my head, like the wordless voices underneath *Daphnis et Chloe*, I'm not sure how to pronounce it, sorry William, get out of my mind, it doesn't matter right now. I'm on a pillowy breast, humming stillness. Like I've not heard before. Like Christmas Eve should have been. Like the womb should have been.

But now trucks honk by on Route 104. I didn't notice them before I climaxed. Passaket, Passaket.

One time William and I drove down here from B.U. to visit Ma, before she got sick. We drove in through Park Square on 104, shot to pothole hell like it always is. But William found it all so delightfully "kitschy-yet-gritty," and tried to make me feel the same. Proud of my heritage! My hometown. The undeniable pull of Nostalgia, he said, dogs of decaying industrialism. Hardened ragged Polish faces and all. And he loved the tough junior-high chicks smoking outside the McDonald's. Oh, Jesus, live with it, Willy. Choke on it. Kitschy crackhouse. Nostalgic racists. Ma.

I can see his face, his reddyblond beard, forming out of the motel dark. Good night, William. See you in the morning.

And now Ma's face, inhuman, mottled like rotten fruit, lying in her self in her bed back home, catheter out, life dripping out. God.

She took care of me in this very city, when I was a kid. And I did come back to take care of her, I did.

Bay State Bombardier

Two goals in this game: fire the ball up the ramp with the top flippers, and shoot it through the tunnels with the main flippers. So I get this rhythm when I alleyoop the ramp and then wing it through Springfield Tunnel, ball comes spinning back out, I'm set up for a ramp shot again. The game's called Bay State Chase. Some local guy invented it.

The only other person in here is the nice old-timer behind the popcorn counter. He senses my pinball rhythm and says, "heh heh," and his garlic breath floats over from across the empty arcade.

***

I grew up in this city. I made all-state forward at Springfield Catholic High, and then I captained Holy Cross College, a few exits down the Mass Pike in Worcester. And though my family's now all either dead or in Florida, I'm still in Springfield, living with a wife in a condo in the nice part of town. I play for the Bay State Bombardiers of the Continental Basketball Association, "one step below the NBA." I know people who would kill to be who I am, a Bay State Bombardier. My name gets in the paper, I make good money, I have health insurance. I have an easier life than most. I don't deny I'm lucky.

"Not for a minute do I deny it, Joy. I'm doing what I love to do, right?" She's stabbing her shredded wheat with a fork and not responding. "But look, I ask you again, do you think I'm doing what I *should* do?"

But Joy just keeps stabbing the goddamn wheat. Then she stands up, and I feel like a slob in the face of her ironed skirt.

"Hey look, I'm sorry, Joy, but I'm one of these people who thinks about what he should be doing with his life, for Christ's sake."

She spins to me on her way to the sink. "Why are you suddenly . . . analyzing everything?"

"What? I thought that's what you liked about me. My searching, or whatever." Sometimes Joy makes me sound like a ten-year-old.

"It's one of the things, but it can't be the only, the only facet of your personality, for God's sake. You lose your focus." She turns to the sink, shoulder blades working. Her blouse has zigzag patterns. "You lose what you're best at."

The game. The goddamn game. "Well, I mean, we're all going to lose it, Joy. I'm starting to lose it, anyway. I mean, I'm twenty-six. Yikes." We've been together six years.

She's palpitating at the drying rack. We should transfer some of her energy on over to me, to even things out. "Look at these . . . *tines*," she says.

"Yeah." I look back to the comics, and everyone's yelling. If it were Sunday, they'd be orange and purple.

She's done with the dishes. "Okay," she says. "Okay, 'bye. I love you."

"I love you. Have a good day at work. There's a. . . . I mean, you're helping on an important case or something, right?"

She breathes. "Don't pretend to be interested in it, because I'm sure not. Just don't play pinball today, okay? Go practice your jump shot. You said you needed to, right? Just don't play pinball."

"Pinball, basketball, what's the difference?"

"Look, just stop it," she says. "Just stop it. Please. Okay, here we go again—anybody can play pinball, only a few people play basketball like you do. Right? So . . . there it is, don't lose it. For God's sake, it's the only reason we're still in Springfield, right?"

She leaves, and I ponder how everything I say sounds like a bad TV show. Maybe I'm watching too many bad TV shows on satellite, in my spare time. Bombardiers have a lot of spare time. I should read more books, like I used to. Or I should practice my jump shot. But it's important to relax.

***

I'm twenty-six and formerly bright, zigging pinballs up ramps and through tunnels. What gives?

The old guy behind the sticky popcorn counter says, "Nailed one, huh?"

The lights stop flashing. "Yeah." I ramp another one, this time for him.

"Who you playing tonight?"

"Albany. Albany. Yeah, Albany Patroons."

***

Springfield War Memorial, where we play, is also where I played big tournament games back in high school, uniting my parents for two hours, which I hated because I knew it wouldn't last. Then game time would come, and I'd zone, and nothing else mattered anymore. Parents were just part of the pulsing blob in the stands. My teammates were my fingertips. I had a triple double here in 1987. The place was packed. Six thousand people, one.

We Bombardiers pull a few hundred a game. Most of the fans in back are good. Focused. They know us. I hear, "Hang in there, Sammy." Sometimes I feel the old vibe buzzing down from the stands up near the piping and catwalks, and I crave for more. But the front rows, suburban and sort-of-rich, always seem pissed. They're angry at having to settle for this minor-league crap while the folks in the Boston office get to impress the clients with luxury-box tickets to Celtics and Bruins games.

Tonight my elbow aches and I'm off again. I miss a couple ten-footers and some second-row goon with a tan and a mustache yells, "What the hell's the matter with this guy, I can do better than him," even though I'm at least playing tough D, even though I did call the switch on the pick. I mean, this Mustache is just goddamn inaccurate. And when I come out of the game he yells, "About fucking time! Your glory days are long gone, Bodwitch!" And he brings his beer to his mouth really slowly and sips it and licks his lips. And I find myself watching the red tongue on mustache and lose my focus. This fucking guy, I've known ones like him all my life roundabout Springfield. I bet he lives in Longmeadow. He's just back from Florida, where he jet-skied, wife-swapped. He's an insurance agent and dreams of ripping me off when I finally get cut from the team, when I finally need to learn about how to buy insurance and stuff like that. When I finally become normal. This Springfield guy and his unfaithful life. Back in high school, I wouldn't have paid him any mind. Coach Mullaney's number three rule: there is no crowd.

The game's over, we won.

Stats-wise, anywise, it's one of my worst nights in four years as a Bombardier. The last five games my shooting has been way out of sync, and Falcone's not going to keep me here just for my defense. But I can't seem to fit in any extra practice. I always end up at the arcade or watching satellite. I've never been this useless. What do you do when you're useless?

My teammates don't hassle me. They're okay; they're just focused on the next level, their NBA wet dream, even here in the small, quiet locker room. I slather on creams and breathe humidity and try to lose myself. My elbow still hurts, though. The trainer says he can't figure it out.

Landry from the *Republican* appears, an intern fresh from the Cross. He knows I'm good for a quote.

He says, "Sam, I figured out that just playing in this league means you're one of the top 750 players in the world. I mean when you figure this is just one step below the NBA."

High on Ben-Gay, I slur, "Oh, what the hell. Hey, friend, this isn't your romantic minor-league baseball, you know? Five players a year, tops, make it to the NBA from this league." The honesty is a buzz, but I shouldn't depress my teammates. So I say, "Look, Landry, why don't we talk about the game? I sucked, but a wild game, hey! A fun game. McCready was a lunatic, a dreadlocked lunatic." I hear McCready, two lockers over, laugh a tad. "And anytime you beat the Patroons, Landry." The ninety-second Ben-Gay burn begins, the part where I'm one with it. "I mean, friend, I'll never get near the NBA, you know it, you *know* Falcone's only got me here to be, what, the local hero, and that's a joke, so . . . let's talk game! This city, right here, Springfield—this is where the game was invented, hey! We've got the Hall of Fame right here! And oh yeah, what the hell's a Patroon?"

Landry stumbles a bit; I came on too hard. Tomorrow in the *Republican* I'll get the following line: "Veteran forward and Springfield hometown hero Sam Bodwitch termed the fourth quarter 'wild and woolly,' and it certainly was that." I won't complain about the misquote.

***

Joy and I met at the Cross, my sophomore year, her senior. She told me that she loved my wholeness, my sonar jump shot complementing my work at the shelter. We ran a food bank together, I passed out supplies and such, I did. Coach DeVito ranted about the time commitment, but I didn't have to listen, because I was the highest-scoring forward they'd had since Tommy Heinsohn. 26.7. Joy and I got our picture in the *Republican* carving a turkey for orphans at Thanksgiving. Local star does good.

I can't say, what, I can't say Joy wasn't my dream-woman or whatever. I mean she jumped right out of this novel I was reading about New York types who are liberal and beautiful and smart. Joy was somehow all of that despite being Catholic. The type of Catholic I never knew in Springfield's hairspray, pot-smoke haze.

When I graduated, the Bombardiers took me in the ninth round, it being hard not to draft a local kid who was twelfth in the country in scoring, even if the Cross is Division Two now and the kid's a tweener. He's a good kid, he's thinking of teaching high school, and his wife's in law school—hell, he might not even come to camp. Let's give him a shot, though, he could put some butts in seats.

So Joy and I finally decided I should try it for a year or so while she finished law school; if it didn't work, we'd go to New York and make lives in her city.

Tonight, four years later, I leave the locker room last, thankful there aren't too many autograph kids to depress me. Sometimes a couple girls hang out, and I get sick and pissed at O'Reilly and Regis for studding them, but late at night, when Joy's asleep and my mind is clogged, I fantasize about the badness of being with those girls.

I sign a quick one for a shuffling guy about my age, and he rends me, because he must be challenged or something, to be asking for an autograph at our age, and to be shuffling like that. I turn around at my car to call him back and connect with him, to show him we're the same, but he's gone.

Instead I see a staring girl, dark on the corner alone. And, well, my shitty game can be an excuse tonight, oh it's a vicious desire, a dirty, a Springfield kid thing, the desire to dirty someone and get away with it, to dirty a lifelong Springfield girl with moussed-up hair and a pout, like seeing a dirty magazine in a bus-station lobby, or in a junior-high bathroom, flash of breast, women holding their own breasts, seeing someone fake pleasure in their dirtiness. I talk to the shadow.

"How you doing?"

"All right," she says.

"You want to come with me?"

As easy as that. I'm a Bombardier. As venal as that. Her name's Michelle.

She turns 19 while we're having sex in Motel 6 on Route 20. The numbers average 15 points a night. But my number game doesn't help me last. I scream every bad word I can think of and grind my hips like an MTV video, bad. Afterwards I'm out-of-my-brains guilty, visioning my shriveled penis on the challenged autograph guy who probably can't control his. And stunned that I'm staying out this late when I have an afternoon game tomorrow.

I take Michelle to the Chicopee Pancake House to happy us both with fluff, but I fade briefly as I recall Mom doing the same for me when I was a kid, this same blue-roofed House, where I marveled at the syrup selection, always assuming there were even more flavors at other tables. Michelle's hair is the color of Imitation Maple and I imagine it gooey in my hands and am ashamed and ask her, "Hey, you want to go play pinball up in Holyoke?"

She sniffs and pulls her head away from her fork. "Where, at Holyoke Arcade?"

"Yeah!"

"No way! You know the old guy that works there? Mickey Ristuccio's uncle?"

"Uh, yeah. You mean the old Italian guy, the popcorn guy."

"Yeah, well, the guy's a flaming faggot. Retard, too."

But I stay nice, and ask much about her life.

"It's all right," she says. "I might take some courses."

I encourage her to do so, and when she quiets, I babble to keep it going. It occurs to me that this is what I've heard a job interview is like, talking and maybe lying just to keep it going, and as the syrup hardens on our forks, I lie.

"Joy's always questioning me about the worth of what I'm doing. Sports are kind of bullshit, aren't they? I mean, when you think about it. So Joy, she thinks maybe I should be doing something more worthwhile."

Michelle snorts and says, "Joy, huh? Joy know you're out with me?"

"No. No. I shouldn't be talking about Joy. Joy and this place don't go together. I used to come here with my mother."

I drive Michelle home nicely to the inevitable West Side crumblies, but finally reach the limit of my niceness at the top of her packed-in street, because I realize we're only two hills over from the one I grew up on. So I refuse to see her house, her parents playing poker or watching the Weather Channel, and I send Michelle walking down the hill. "Take it easy, kid."

"Yeah, right."

Her tough two-syllable *yeah* sticks with me all the way home as I flee the mass of ugly old Springfield three-families and tree-cracked streets, back to our cute new development, where I can still hear Michelle in bed, in between Joy's breathing.

Joy and I smell like people, kind of sour and sticky, and though I don't want to have sex as I'm drained from Michelle, I realize I love Joy for a minute.

I joggle her a bit and squeeze her hand and say, "Joy, I'm sorry we fought. I'm sorry we fought. This morning."

She murmurs, "Sorry I couldn't make the game."

"That's okay."

"How'd it go."

"We won, but I was shit."

"You didn't shoot well," she says into the pillow.

"Right."

"But . . . how was your defense? Did you focus?"

Her hair is unruly, tickling me. Imperfect. Maybe she'll understand. "Listen, Joy. Try to understand. I have to be honest with you—I don't know how much longer the hoops is going to last. I'm just not good enough anymore."

She breathes steadily and lightly. I think she's asleep, and I wonder if I'm going to have to say this again another time, but she finally whispers, "It's okay, it's okay."

"Mm. I'm a good person, though, and I'm going to find something good to do with my life." I sound like a movie again, but I think I really mean it. "Something better than sports. I just . . . I hope you're not disappointed that I'm not, you know, exactly the person you fell in love with."

She says something. I think it's "go to sleep."

In the morning, I'll call the career office at the Cross, maybe they help alums. Or I'll go to the library downtown and look at job books or something. Maybe someone there can show me how to use the Internet better, and I can find a career that way. I need to learn how to use that thing.

***

But I wake up at 10, hard from dreaming of Michelle. Only three hours till our Wednesday matinee, and on a place mat in the kitchen Joy has left today's *New York Times*. She insists on getting it even though we also get the *Republican*. She's stuck a post-it note on the *Times* saying, "Check out page D8, good article." It's some poetic sportswriter jerking off over minor-league baseball and its *wonderful lingo, all playful razzing and chirps*, a paean to a guy who made it to the majors at age thirty-two after fourteen years in the bushes. *All grit and sideways spits.* The article makes stomach juice rise up my throat, but later I'll tell Joy it was well-written. Something's snatching me away from Joy and the *Times*, though. Michelle's moussey smell and pursed lips as we ground together. And I comprehend suddenly the vastness of what Joy doesn't know about me, what I haven't told her about certain hates and loves I've developed.

I'm bulging from Michelle. Realizing that she slept with me only because I'm halfway famous gives me the same type of hard-on I got behind the dumpster out back of the Cumberland Farms, age twelve, reading the surplus XXX's they threw out at the end of the month. I want to think about Michelle, her flat voice, like I used to talk, her crinkly chemical hair, think about her and masturbate on the *New York Times*. I must admit all of this. I can feel guilty later.

I throw out the sogged newspaper and turn on a satellite channel with the Hollywood Squares and start drinking ancient Narragansett that I found in the storage space. I've never drunk before a game, ever. It's not fair to the fans. Mullaney would kill me if he were alive. It's unconscionable. I bet Michelle's done some unconscionable things.

And now I'm lubed, and it's 1978 on TV because the Squares all have perms, and they're making jokes about Jimmy Carter and *Three's Company*, my childhood, JoJo White my Celtics hero, he dribbles through Paul Lynde and the energy crisis in the middle square, JoJo quiet, focused, contained, veteran, ultimate teammate, perpetual motion, and I think, "I'll play through this for Michelle, I'll play right through the middle of this and out the other side, playing is the way to get through any problem." All my coaches have said that. I finish the six-pack. Playing is the way to get through any problem.

And this afternoon, somehow, I am through it. Today's game is for Michelle, I can feel her heat in the misty War Memorial. And I sense a promise of a post-game treat. Coach puts me in at the start of the second quarter, and I drain three in a row, flowing like yesteryear. The elbow's numb and I'm lubed and not worrying about anything. I smell Cream of Wheat and dry tea bags from when I was a kidster watching Hollywood and JoJo and I'm eight years old, out on the court alone with hazy smiling teammates and baffled opponents. At a timeout I know what Coach will X and O before he draws it. "Those goofy fools in the enemy uniforms," I tell McCready. "Listen, they're stuck in gooey wheat, hey, but I'm floating around on a Mister Clean boat." It sounds like it rhymes even though it doesn't.

"Whatever," McCready says, "whatever you're on. Just keep making the shots."

We're back out and I miss one but then say what the hell and step behind the line and arc a dead-on three-pointer, which not even JoJo could do 'cause they didn't have three-pointers back then, I'm *creating* the game, I'll take it all on, and at halftime, so as not to lose it, I snap my fingers and bop around the locker room, slapping hands with Regis and McCready.

Coach says, "Okay, looks like Bodwitch is our man today, four for five so far. Bodwitch, they're going to be all over you now, so when you get in there find the open man on the rotate."

"I'm there, Coach, I'm there, I'll feed them, feed you like a baby, Regis," I pat this alien kid from the Bronx and we actually connect for a second, I think.

I get to start the third quarter and immediately knock down a couple more twelve-footers, so they double-team me, so I feed Turco and then McCready on a cut for two and it counts, and then finally it seems their entire defense converges on me as I drive left, and I reinvent this pass from when I was ten at the playground five miles from here and I hadn't even played on a team yet, hadn't even thought about sex yet, just me and five other kids shooting funball after school in dark December, snow dust on the ground, yes, driving so hard baseline, magnetizing the whole defense over to me because I'm so *on*, then at the last second flicking my off-wrist for a no-look bounce pass, slipping it just behind their backs and minds, it bounces flat on the lane box and up to McCready as the whole frantic defense lands with me in the out-of-bounds, crashing through wires and cheerleaders and front-row season-ticket-holder cynics, back on the court McCready takes it, undulates, lay it up and in, Jackie Dreadlocked Kid, smooth, all day I gave you, took them all away from you, kiss it off the glass, take all your time. I feel a hand reach down from the cheap-seat rafters and I smile up towards it, right.

Right. But goddamn it. What is it, this basketball feeling? Is it supposed to ever last? Does it mean a goddamn thing?

Because when I untangle from the crowd, my elbow suddenly hurts like hell. I think I cracked it on a chair, and I carry the pain back to the floor. I taste beer in my burp. The game hasn't stopped, and they're down at the other end, and there's something wrong with my elbow. I get the ball, but they're on me so quick I bounce it off my foot. I make a steal, but I'm tired and throw the pass away. Some smudge stands up behind our bench and yells, "What the hell kind of a pass was that?" Could be any one of fifty Mustaches over there. Could be the same guy from last night. It is. I see his red, glistening tongue, licking hairs. The ball flies past my face.

My eyes are watering, and I take off my goggles and it all melts. I know I'm never going to play really well again.

I say to McCready while someone's shooting fouls, "Where the hell. . . . Where the hell does that guy get off, man? Yelling at me. I mean have I not had an excellent game? I mean, does he just *refuse* to see that?"

McCready's rubbing the bottoms of his sneakers. "Oh, man, you're going to start listening to those shits?" He jerks his middle finger over towards the guy. "Wasn't it you who told me last year not to even think about them? When the shits called me *nigger*?"

I think. "Yeah, I guess that was me."

Whatever was working is gone. I'm thick in the throat, playing in steam and can't see the ball, can see only my gullet clogged from morning alcohol and mustache hair, and sweet, sweet Michelle, whom I now realize probably isn't at this matinee at all but is rather temping nine-to-five in an office park, getting her act together, thinking about taking classes, becoming responsible.

"Jesus Christ, look at Bodwitch! I can play better than this guy! He's had his famous days, get him out of there!"

Finley's at the scorer's table ready to replace me. A rock in my gut. I take the rock in a blur on a weave and I whirl and fire it at that bastard's mustache. The ball ricochets off some kid's head and out of my vision, maybe into Mustache's Lap, because I hear, "Hey! My fucking beer!"

Coach grabs me on my way to the locker room. "What the hell was that?"

"That's it, Coach. I guess."

***

On my way up to Holyoke I pass the dead and looming PlasticsPlus plant. I remember when it closed, junior year of high school, because my buddy Colwell had to leave the team when his father transferred to Orlando.

I pass drug deals on the dampened corners and maybe some sex, too, but I try to focus on the pinball.

You know, I could have sold drugs in this city, I could have dug ditches. I could have taught high school.

I'm not going to be able to play pinball today, am I? The flippers will seem slack and my timing will be off. Oh Christ, if it ends, and I think it has, Joy will say, after long pauses, okay. It's a shame. It's a shame. You were a great player, you loved the game. But life can go on. We should move to New York now. There are opportunities in New York, for her especially, but me too. She'll show me the city ropes. Let's be honest, Springfield *is* dead. It's Joy's turn now. I had my few years, a couple of decent ones. It's Joy's turn now, only fair.

I pull a U-Turn and head down to the Hall of Fame instead of pinball. I'm hoping to shoot a bunch at the "History of

Rims" they have on the bottom floor, where you can shoot hundreds of balls from a moving walkway. I've always wanted to fire away for hours at the peach baskets, wooden backboards, plexiglasses. I know I'll hit at least one groove if I stay awhile. Even with my elbow, I know I'll eventually nail ten in a row. I can impress the tourists.

But when I get to the Hall, I'm surrounded by challenged people, heaving the balls at one another's faces and chairs. Their caretakers have brought them here on a dead Wednesday afternoon, hoping there won't be any mocking kids to torture them. There aren't any kids, but still, the challenged people are making dying-cow noises and bashing themselves and each other. One's laughing. Some of them are crying. Challenged. Retards. Fuck-ups. Challenged.

I'm going to leave forever. But at the exit there's a little display. In town for the Basketball Hall of Fame? Come see *live* basketball with Springfield's own Bombardiers. CBA Action, one step below the NBA. I'm third in from the left in the team picture. 6'5", shiny uniform, halfway famous. Health insurance, good money, lawyer wife. People would kill to be me.

Self-Righteous Pedant

It's late Sunday morning, and the Assignment Committee has miraculously neglected to schedule me for miscreant-supervising or dorm-surveillance duties. My bowels surge at the promise of freedom, and I determine to lose myself in lunch and the Celtics at a Pittsfield pub. Jumping into my fishbowl of a car, I flee campus the secret way, up the rocky access road.

But skinheaded, steel-toed Bean is skulking about the historic-landmark barn on the edge of school property, hard by Route 20. I accelerate as my stomach seizes. Bean espies me and dashes into the road, his oft-professed disregard for his own life proven by his willingness to jump in front of my car. I've no choice but to slow down.

He leaps onto the hood and pounds the windshield. "You *have* to bring me, Mr. Hoffman," he howls, splotching his face against the glass. "I don't know where you're going, but you *have* to bring me."

He's a terribly bright but utterly wrecked kid from Seattle who snorts crushed No-Doz when he can't obtain illegal stimulants. *Wealthy yet troubled*, our target student profile, though Bean's more troubled than most. If I let him come with me, I lose any hope for a glimmer of peace.

"Get in the car, Bean." Inevitable. I'm enslaved to my visceral desire to *make the kids like me.* Or maybe it's just Shaker kindness.

The Discipline Committee has forced Bean to dig drainage ditches for the last month. His venom is well stewed, and he spews it out all the way over the mountain to Pittsfield, fouling the interior of my car.

"Fucking morons!"

"Watch your language," I snap reflexively, discharging a semblance of duty.

"And you're a hypocrite, Hoffman! Most Popular Teacher bullshit—you don't do anything to help!"

"Come on, Bean."

"They make me dig ditches—you think that's just?"

"Of course it's not just!" I disapprove morally of Bean's steel-toed, tail-cutting rampages, but these rampages are not why he's digging ditches; indeed, the DC members tacitly encourage such macho forays. Instead, they punish Bean for *accumulated black marks*: one for being late for check-in, three for swearing at a teacher, etc.

But trying to explain the complexity of all this to Bean triggers some remnant notion of being honor bound never to criticize my colleagues, so I encode my explanation in *weird words.* "You know, Bean, it does truly rankle me that your judges are petty, uh . . . you know, their petty opiate revelries, their perfunctory infidelities. . . . But I shouldn't judge them, either. Let's just say I'm embarrassed by it all, and of course they shouldn't punish you."

"What the hell are you talking about? Mr. Shaker. Mr. Weird Words. Mr. Holy-of-Holies."

"So I'm holier than thou, huh? Well, that's not a sin," I say, realizing right away that, technically, it is.

"They make me dig ditches. It's a joke and they treat me like shit and . . . yeah-yeah, shit!"

"I'm going to have to give you a black mark for language, Bean!"

He laughs, turns on his Walkman, and begins to emit a continuous Arabic wail as accompaniment. I brood on the loss of the redemptive potential that I pathetically assigned to this excursion. Aside from the esteem accorded me by my students, my eighteen months of living and working at Shaker Heritage School have been an unmitigated disaster, and I persevere only to experience those rare moments in which I can escape campus. I've long harbored the dream of living and teaching in the Shaker tradition—celibate, rural, contemplative, pacifistic—but the dream won't materialize at Heritage. "No one else here gives a shit about the Shakers," say my colleagues, who consider me *dark*, *smart*, and woefully ignorant of the benefits of collegiality. Last month, one of them even sputtered that I was a *self-righteous pedant*. "Big words for you," I mumbled.

We pull up to Jimmy's Roadside and walk towards the lounge. From outside, I see the four little green booths, empty, and four or five people at the bar. And the Celtics, green-and-white on TV, beaming to Pittsfield from the Fleet, three hours away on the Pike. Back home. A scene that would give me two hours of peace were it not for this miserable kid by my side. Suddenly I grab him by the door and hiss, "You are going to behave yourself in there. You are going to watch the game, and you will have something to eat, and you will . . . behave like a human. You got me?" The colloquialized interrogative is an attempt to add an element of toughness missing from my usual pedantic parlance.

Bean's biceps snap tight in my grip, and I suffer a quick vision of the possessed Bean sweating in his room, his Korean roommates babbling incoherence, Bean flexing thousands of pull-ups on a grimy bar, preparing for final conflict.

"Yeah, I *got* you," he says through his nose. "But you know you can't control me, Hoffman." He grins slightly.

I unhand him. "I mean it."

We enter, and I tell Bean to order whatever he wants, hoping to precipitate a goodwill exchange. Meanwhile, the game is blurring by on the sets. I yearn for one bleeding-in moment with these subtle Celtics fans. To become one of and with them. I beg God for mercy, for just a glint of that holy feeling that the Celtics gave me when I was an unknowing boy, ensconced in my bedroom with my little TV.

Bean will have none of any of it. I've gleaned only that it's the beginning of the second quarter and that the Celtics are winning when he spits, "So here we are in a *bar*, watching a *game*—why aren't you out like a Shaker feeding the *poor*, Mr. Hoffman? Mr. Holy Mr. Hoffman?"

"I do feed the poor, Bean. Every Tuesday down in Stockbridge." I hate lying like this, losing control. "You ever wonder why I'm not on campus on Tuesdays? Now watch the game."

A commercial blares.

"Basketball, Bean, my sport," I blather. "Non-violent, team-oriented. And here we have the Celtics *beating the Mavericks* on a Sunday. This is incredibly significant. They haven't beaten the Mavericks in *three years*, Bean. Much less on a Sunday, which is their worst day." I sound like I'm making fun of myself. Either that, or I sound absurdly earnest about something that Bean obviously deems pathetic, as indicated by his slit-eyed, lip-curling visage. A visage that we both know implies, "You value this? You, the liberal, serious history teacher, the basketball coach who says winning doesn't matter, you value a bunch of guys in shorts making millions of dollars from throwing a ball in a ring?" He says it all in a smirk, I don't need to hear it.

"I mean, do you know the significance, Bean? This is like the Allies establishing a second front, or something," I say, making reference to last week's lesson, making it all a joke, smearing the meaning out of it.

The food arrives, entirely too quickly. Bean stares at a forkful of obviously microwaved Newburg slop, then at me, then back at the slop incredulously while orbiting the fork above his Coke, and I let him play, and tension builds, and I sniff-laugh involuntarily at both the tension and his look of caricatured disbelief, instead of doing my job, which is to say, "Don't play with your food, Bean." I know the pattern: the imp toys with the line between comic playfulness and ripe repugnance, somehow making me complicit in whatever might follow. And now he's smearing the pinkish-white goo on his cheeks, and letting it fall slowly out of his mouth, and moaning, "I'm eating Jews, Mr. Hoffman, want some? Jew Shakers! That's all there is to eat, you gotta make do. Want some mashed Jew Shaker?" Somehow merging brilliantly two of my recent lessons, one on the Holocaust, the other on starvation in Stalin's gulags. He's unspeakably offensive by any imaginable standards, and I hear the inevitable Only Woman at the bar say, "My God, that's so disgusting. Jesus God. . . ."

Things are spinning apart. "Stop that, Bean," I gibber. "I'm not kidding. Stop that or you're in serious trouble."

"What are you going to do, go to Spooch?"

He knows that going to Spooch, the Director of Discipline, will accomplish nothing besides making me vomit. I'll try to explain to Spooch the immorality of Bean's transgression, and the veteran, Aryan, sturdy, beloved, moronic lacrosse coach Spooch will ask, "Did he commit any black marks?"

"No," I'll be forced to reply, since anti-Semitism and food-smearing are not explicitly listed in the Student Handbook under *Black Marks*.

"Well, don't complicate things, Hoffman. You know . . . you can't jump at every little incident." Spooch.

I murmur to Bean, "Yeah. Yeah, Spooch is a real jerk, real hypocrite, isn't he."

"There you go, Hoffman! They're all hypocrites, but not you. Yeah, you stand alone. The Mover and the Shaker!" He follows this volley with a jowly horror-movie laugh that causes some of the speckled Newburg to fall off of his cheeks.

Nauseous and bewildered, I stare at the complex lunatic. His criticisms have no moral thrust, right? But they almost always seem accurate, and maybe intelligent.

Intelligent Bean now picks up a handful of pink, dripping slop, and says, "Shaker Jew." The complexity of it all threatens to explode me.

The bartender appears. He knows I'm from Heritage, and he likes me when I'm alone. But he won't *cut me any slack*. He *gets in my face*. "This kid's making people sick, Hoffman. If you can't control him, you're out of here. And I'll call your headmaster and have the whole damn school booted from here for a month."

"Okay, I'm sorry, I'm sorry." I nod to show that I *know*, I'm in touch with him. I know what's normal. He shakes his head and goes back to the bar.

"Now *you're* in trouble, Hoffman," says Bean, the slop making mud noises as it goops onto the plate.

A minor roar from the bar. The Celtics must be doing something remarkable, against Dallas, on a Sunday. But I'm missing it all, and everything's so damn unfair.

These words spill out: "Bean, listen. Listen. What's something you really want?"

"To be free!"

"No, I mean what's something I can give you?"

"Give me an A in your class. If I get an A, my father will buy me the gun I want. It's a copycat Uzi with a—"

"All right, listen. I'll give you an A. You know I don't care about grades anyway. I'll give you an A for this marking period if you just go to the bathroom, wash up, and then be quiet for twenty minutes. Okay?"

"You won't give me an A."

"No, no, I will. I promise. Look." I pick up the steak knife, unaware of what I'll do with it. "I'll cut myself—"

"What?"

I growl, "I'll cut myself to prove it," and I cup my hands, turn my back to the bar, and jab the serrated knife into my hidden palm. A strange dull pain ensues, not the sting that I expected. For a moment I'm unsure of time and place, and I receive a flash of last night's dream, which featured magic marching Nazis dancing with Shakers. Then Bean, pointing at my palm, makes a low moan that sounds like an unsuccessful attempt to pronounce a *g*.

"See?" I say. "See what I do? Now just go clean up, and be quiet." And I jiggle my head in a consciously crazy style, thinking Bean might relate and appreciate. "And when you come back, just be quiet, truly quiet, for twenty minutes, and you get an A." A red circle begins to form in my palm, not bleeding, just pulsing. We both stare at it.

"Okay, Sarge," he says, *at least a little bit scared of me*, I think.

Bean gets up and I look around—has anyone seen my stabbing? They're all watching the game; the woman glances darkly at Bean as he saunters towards the bathroom. I nibble at some horribly salty fried clams.

A chance at camaraderie. Wadding up a napkin in my palm, I try to make a quick study of the game, and say to the bar, "Is Blount in there because Battie is in foul trouble, or, uh

... is he just resting?" A black-eyed guy turns and just twists his mouth at me. The twist says, "Where do you get off bringing that goddamn maniac sicko in here?"

The sicko's back, talking even as he sits down. "I'm not going to play your grade games, Mr. Hoffman," he enunciates. "I'll talk if I want to talk, and I'll say what I want to say. The hell with your grades."

"Bean . . . Bean . . . Bean, I'm nice enough to bring you down here, on my day off, and you just treat me like . . . crap, you know." Not a word I use often, and I brace for ridicule. But all I get is a taste of salty residue from behind my teeth. "Listen, I'm just going to drive us back to campus, Bean. I don't feel well."

But as I begin to raise my hand to ask for the check, he grabs my wrist firmly and says, "No. Please." And he laughs slightly, a laugh that an objective observer might actually deem sincere and self-effacing.

"Don't squeeze the blood out of my hand hole," I mumble.

He relaxes the grip and says, "Okay. But listen, I can't go back to that . . . hell. *Please*, Hoffman."

"Uh-huh. Uh-huh." I close my eyes.

But his tone is strangely genuine. "No, *please*, Mr. Hoffman." He lets go. I open my eyes, and his palms are spread in a gesture of peace.

"Listen, Bean . . . I hate it there, too." Faculty aren't allowed to say that. My hand pulses, my stomach swishes. "I hate Heritage, too, but, you know, there's nothing that can be done without . . . breaking several laws." I get a snapshot vision of Bean and I just never going back to Heritage, just establishing some sort of a partnership here in Pittsfield, a little office, dispensers of lore, or something. Or zooming somewhere, everywhere, telling the world our story.

"Look, Hoffman, I only came here with you today because I figured you'd help me. You're the only one. Just bring me to the train station, Hoffman—"

"Oh, no. Don't ask me that, don't."

"No, really." His eyes shine. "I swear to God I won't *tell* anyone you brought me. I just can't go back to fucking Heritage. Please. They treat me like shit, you know, they laugh at me, they say I'm useless because I don't fucking play sports . . . and it just turns me into more of a maniac."

I must spit, spit a little Coke into my napkin. *Set Bean free.* How can something so right be so completely illegal? "Listen, Bean, listen, I hate it there, too. I hate it there, too. They're so mean to me." Then I break many rules and say, "Bean . . . why don't you just bolt, Bean? Just run out that door. I won't look."

"Because I don't know where the damn train station is. I don't know where anything is in this . . . this *state*."

True. Sincere. The train station is ten miles away, hidden out near Dalton. He'd never find it. He'd be picked up as a transient.

And now, through my haze, I see that Bean has changed. He glows. Damn it—*Set Bean Free!* Because if I don't, all I'll ever see is a mean-but-miserable, lonely, fuzzy kid, stranded in these terminal Berkshires, surrounded by nothing but jocks, cokeheads, and cockroaches. And me. Me the only one to save him. Look, sometimes the world must offer legitimate opportunities to do good. Offer responsibility. I have to believe that, anyway. I refuse to live in a nihilistic universe. "Nihilism sucks, Bean."

"Why won't you just *do* this?" His voice is getting too loud again. "No one saw you leave campus with me!"

That's most likely true. Yes, I see, I see how easy it would be to just let this kid free in the vibrant universe, pregnant with potential. To do my part. Once I do my part, it'll be someone else's turn.

"I won't *tell*," he hisses, "listen, I won't *tell*." He glows more brightly, expands, then grabs the knife and begins sawing away at his hand. The skin moves like rubber and then breaks.

I throw down some money and yank him outside.

"Let's go . . . out awhile. Maybe we go out awhile," I murmur, pushing him towards the car.

We drive twenty minutes in a silence broken only by Bean humming and sucking on his bleeding knuckles. I drop him off behind the massive, long-dead GM Plant in the middle of nowhere. No one's ever here, no one sees us. The train station is about a half-mile away, and I explain the route.

When I finish, I say, "Okay, Bean . . . okay. . . ."

Bean, out of the car now and grinning, leans through my window and says, "You'll be all right, Mr. Hoffman. No one saw us leave campus." I smell acrid Newburg stationed in his craw. A thin slicemark sparkles across his hand.

"But . . . your hand, Bean. And you don't have any money! How are you going to buy a ticket?"

"I've got like six credit cards. We all do, all us students. We're not poor like you. Don't you know that?" And the laugh returns. Glorying in the sickness of it all, I suppose. But maybe that's not all. Maybe he's happy because I'm setting him free.

"Bean," I say. "Bean, Bean. So pristine. Ha ha." I should rub his fuzzy skinhead goodbye. I watch him dance his way down an access road, between two huge, dead, pink buildings.

Alone now, I drive around the Berkshires, not listening to the Celtics' post-game show. I notice the wind and look up at dusky Monument Mountain, off of which Indians and a Shaker or two used to hurl themselves in order to please gods. People with purposes. "I grew up at the complete other end of this state, Bean," I say to the car. "I'm an alien, too." Where will the train bear Bean? Will his parents or the school sue me if they find out what I've done? I try not to care.

I finally return to campus for 9:00 Evening Meeting.

At which I hear about Bean. He never made it to the train station. Around 7:30, the Dalton Comfort Inn called Spooch to pick up a drunken Bean, who'd taken a room, trashed it, and then "caused a scene" in the restaurant.

He told Spooch that he'd hitchhiked to Dalton. No mention of Mr. Hoffman. I should go thank Bean for saving me, but they have him in *solitary*, no visitors allowed.

In my dorm room on the fifth floor of a crumbling, centuries-old, Official Landmark, I wonder about Bean. I guess he's out of my hands now, in someone else's.

Post-Meeting on Sunday night is traditionally the *serious party time* for off-duty faculty, but they seem to have reached a particularly convulsive pitch tonight. Bean's rampage and subsequent capture comprise a Big Event, and the off-duties shoot and eat a wild turkey and drink Wild Turkey in the ancient Meeting House where the Shakers used to pray. My refusal to attend is mocked with rude, giggling phone calls. I swear to myself that I am above it all.

But I'm not. I don't fit, but I'm part of the whole hell. Bean's imprisoned, and I'm doing nothing. I'm a hypocrite. Bean, Bean, so damnably accurate.

Husbands sleep with others' wives tonight. All are drunk. Maybe it shouldn't bother me but what can I say, I'm a self-righteous pedant, for better or worse. The hedonism infecting that holy white Meeting House sickens me. Paper-correcting, treadmill, stationary bike, and still I can't sleep. Never before such loathing, both of self and others. Forever I've held that I do *good work*. Even if others call me a goody two-shoes, and self-righteous—the work remains. Yet it all seems shat away tonight at Shaker Heritage School. Why *aren't* I out feeding the poor?

It's too late to feed them tonight. Frenzied revel sounds drift across campus. I must do something tonight.

I go down to the south edge of campus, down behind the dairy barn to the faculty parking lot, away from the dorms, away from lives. Dead Shakers howl in the wind.

It feels right, swinging my arms out here in the rural air I've always coveted. When I swing the bat at the Shaker Heritage School motto sticker, "*Hands to Work, Hearts to God,*" on the rear window of Spooch's car, the Spoochglass shatters while the sticker stays whole. Liberating the Shakers, and maybe Bean along with them, is morally precise.

I know that smashing windows on drunken colleagues' cars is arbitrary. But I also affirm the potential efficacy of the act. Carried out properly, it forces those cocky, complacent libertines to confront the spectre of cosmic justice. That's the way I feel, that's who I am. If I admit I'm self-righteous, then at least I won't be a hypocrite.

***

Two days later, the Discipline Committee expels Bean for bashing faculty-car windows.

I justify my silence at the hearing by ruminating, "He'll be better off away from this place, anyway," even though his parents have decided to send him to a psychiatric hospital in Miami. At least the drugs will be legal there. And paying for the windows is no burden for them.

But. But But. I left him out to dry. Didn't I.

For expulsions at Heritage, we conduct an insane ceremony in which the faculty all go to the Room of Brethren and stand in two rows wearing berets while the exiled kid, bareheaded, walks past us down the aisle. Somehow it's supposed to communicate to the deviant that we're not totally disowning him, that he'll be welcomed back to our community of scholars, if and when he ever rehabilitates himself "—and if of course tuition is paid in full." We stage the ceremony only if the pariah agrees to it, which Bean apparently has.

I'm at the end of a row because I'm the newest faculty member—tradition. Bean has to stand at the beginning of the rows next to the veterans while Spooch sings "Simple Gifts," the Shaker theme song, a paean to simplicity, humility, and reverence. "'Tis a gift to be simple, 'tis a gift to be free." He sings it *basso profundo*, powerful, a *good voice* that makes everyone smile, because you need a *good voice* to sing *good songs*, regardless of how fascist you are, oh God I want to vomit, I want to disgorge and die, and now I catch Bean's eye, and he smiles, but a sad smile, knowing how sick we all are.

Spooch finishes, "by turning, turning, we come 'round right." Faculty shake their heads in wonderment at the profundo. I'm considering the ramifications of saying something. Will they understand me? Will they just further ostracize the self-righteous pedant? Will God listen?

Bean's steel toes walk by me. He's at the front door. I run to him and toss my beret to the floor with an overstatedly free motion.

"Bean. I'm sorry." He turns towards me, and I put my hand on his skinhead. His bristles prickle my sore as I look back at the faculty. "Let it be known," I say. "Just . . . let it be known. . . ."

Peace Garden

There was a smiley tourist trap up on the borderline. International Peace Garden. North Dakota-Manitoba border strewn with flower clocks, flag plantings, peace alfalfa.

Me and my buddy Smarm hated the tourist slime. Tourists were buckeyes and plaids and tootles and golf bags, and "rich enough to cruise the country, dumb enough to look like that," said Smarm. Me and Smarm were somewhat cool, cooler at least than the tourists and the beery farm boys and crewcuts we'd grown up with. We sang "shade-sporting, glue-snorting," and did no one's thing but ours. Smarm even pretended to be Indian and sort of looked it, growing his hair like wires, like the Indians over to the reservation.

One day Smarm got himself banned from the county community college for trying to put fire to the baseball team uniforms. I saw him crying, black-teared from the stuff he painted 'round his eyes. I didn't know what to say, both of us feeling like crap. I'd been feeling old at age twenty, fading in and out all day, something wrong with my head workings. I was scared of the rest of my life. Working in a freaking Dairy Dream. And then maybe after five years, what, *managing* the freaking Dairy Dream. I knew that there were people worse off, in cities and China or wherever, but I was focused on me and my lot. The farm boys at least *owned* something, a farm, or at least they would when their parents died. And the crewcuts who'd gone off to the service were all set, as long as they stayed in for twenty years. Pensions. Set for life at age thirty-eight, Jesus. While I'd still be Dairy Dreaming. But I could never make it in the service, because I don't like getting yelled at.

With all of this in my mind and Smarm embarrassed from crying, we tried to turn ourselves around and get ragged and raging. We sniffed a couple sneebies for to help us along the way. After a couple minutes, the sneebies blasted through to our brains and we decided, on Smarm's suggestion, to go kick a ruckus up on the line.

Smarm was erupting next to me as I drove, spewing the way it would be. "This is the way it'll be, it'll be, I been waiting to do this, we're going to the Peace Garden Chapel, Joker, we'll set off a smokey delay. I got *rez* smokeys, Joker, *rez*." He held up the plastic baggie full of stink bombs, little black bean things. Wild Indian stink-bomb delays, once you unwrapped them they took ten minutes to smoke fully. Opened slow like a flower.

"We're the men, Smarm. We'll wake up all the bozos."

"*Really*, though, Sickie, listen," and he catapulted some tale at me that I could maybe halfway follow, something about how he'd swapped a bag of weed for a copy of the Peace Chapel's maintenance plan from some guy who worked there for a week, I don't know, there was a lot more to it. Smarm put all his energies into figuring out plans and deals like these, and then I'd get to go along for the fun. Somehow he hadn't burned out quite as fast as I had, there was still this fuse in him that could burn for hours if it got lit by the right sneebie. And I must say this about Smarm, aside from anything else: he never complained about having to do all the figuring, and he did always call me Joker or Sickie or even buddy, which was cool.

"I'm going to set it in the back roo, the back room, no one can see—oh man, I've got it *all* figured this time—ten minutes later it'll hit the sprinks off, *all* the sprinks'll go off in the whole place, it'll piss water all over their fuzzy heads, and the fire doors'll whip open so they'll get hit with the stink, too!" We'd tried something like that one time before, in high school, so as to wreck the sports award ceremony, and though someone had smelled the smoke stink early and gotten everyone out before the sprinks had sprunk, we'd had a fine old time watching the jockheads bolt and pyew. I hated those jock bastards, with their ties on and hair washed to receive their medals from the principal and their prayers from the minister, good straight-arrow boys, and then they'd head on over to a rented house in Minot to rape drunken ninth-graders and brag about it on Monday. I can't say I wouldn't have done the same if I'd had the chance, but I was never any good at sports—something about no depth perception. So I didn't rape anybody, and I think I should get credit for that regardless of the reasons.

We stormed up County Road 12, breaking all limits in my brickhead brother's Buick. Smarm kept raging, but I faded. Slicing the edge of Dawson Farm and the reservation, we kicked up a huge brown dust cloud, in which I saw berry-picking with Dad and Sunday hikes. I was seven years old once, I was clean once. But then I saw slightly later smears of dirt-biking and pot-sucking and shooting up with Smarm by lonely thick trees and busted-out tractors and things, my life dead-ended in a dust cloud, my sinuses clogged from it and tears starting to crinkle. No, I never raped anybody or got drunk; that was for the jockheads I hated, and the farm boys, and some of the crewcuts, and the ones who were all three.

But I did grow up in my own sick way, getting stoned a lot. At least that was *different* from the others. I guess that's why I started smoking pot and sniffing glue, and then later crushing little caps and pills and snorting them up my nose. I knew it wasn't good for me, but I did it anyway. It set me apart from the jocks and the rest. We were all sick in some way, all of us fine young men in Rolette County.

I faded back into reality at the borderline check on 281. It wasn't quite eight o'clock, so we just caught the end of Old Green Borderman's shift. He hated us "weirdos," me fat and glassy-eyed, Smarm trying to look like Geronimo. We weren't good local boys with shotguns and a pick-up, we were just weirdos with a Buick. He made us step out and open the rusty trunk and everything, while meantime a couple trucks of bombed bozos just waved on through to Huntin' Land. They probably had enough guns to wipe out the whole country, but Border Asshole was more interested in our trunk. He was mumbling, "Look at this damn mess in here," as he rummaged through my brother's flashlights and comic books and got his damn greasy hands on my banjo strings. But I didn't say anything because I didn't want any trouble; the one thing I still really liked to do was drive up to Canada alone after work sometimes and just cruise through the little towns and farms of another country at twilight time. So I needed Borderman's goodwill. Old Green Borderman, he probably had his own damn Canadian pension, they treat everyone like kings up there. Where the hell they get the money I don't know, maybe it's because they don't have to pay for a decent army. Maybe I should have moved up to Canada and gotten a pension. A pension without having to go into the service, good deal.

Well, there was nothing illegal in the car, we'd stuck it all into our noses and the stink bombs down the back of Smarm's t-shirt, so Borderman came up empty and had to let us in. We threw the banjo in the back seat, then Smarm threw Old Green Borderman the finger as we pulled off. This finger meant I'd have to go twenty miles out of my way to the border station over at Hansboro for the next few months so as to avoid a scene with Old Green, who worked both Rolette stations. And so I was quite pissed at Smarm, but as usual I didn't say anything, because I didn't want to lose my only buddy.

We reached the Peace Garden inside of a couple minutes. Then we took the Canadian loop through the Garden to the Chapel, driving through rows of cooperatively planted Peace Pines. Again I blanked for a bit as Smarm bubbled something. I had a headache, and sniffing out the window at the springy air only shot some more pain to my temples. My whole person wasn't working. "What the hell," I wondered, "is becoming the matter with me?" I took another sneebie snort but just got a screwdriver stab right through to the middle of my brain. You can only take so many.

We parked fifty feet from America by the side of the Peace Chapel, a big yellow-brick doughnut with red jelly spots for the doors. Some service songs seeped out, smiley stuff like "Give Peace a Chance."

"What a bunch of hypo-pricks," snorked Smarm. "Give peace a fricking chance, then they'll . . . drop bombs on the rez. Or something."

"Yeah." I was recalling the time that Smarm had gone over to the rez because he'd heard they had the best weed, and he claimed to have some Indian blood so he figured they'd like him and give him a good deal, but as it turned out they just knocked the crap out of him and called him "white boy." For a while after that, he didn't pretend to be Indian anymore. But eventually he decided to make believe he'd forgotten that they'd beaten him up. I wanted to remind him now. I was getting sick of Smarm and had to admit it to myself. He said the same crap over and over and smelled like an old, pot-infested shoe. I'm sure I did too, but I didn't notice.

Smarm ran in to plant the bomb. He jobbed open the door to what looked like the boiler room, I don't know. I was way too stuffed and throbbing to wonder. With Smarm gone, the air in the car cleared a bit. I closed my eyes and heard the droning chaplain, who soon became lost in someone peeing, peeing baby and soft. The pain eased a bit. Opening my eyes I realized the pee sound was the tiny waterfall of the Healing Peace Stream, planted by the Winnipeg Women's Club. A pebbly, smiley stream, with a couple of crutches, knee supports, a brace propped against a rock, it's a cluttery world.

Smarm reappeared. "It's all set. I stuck near ten of the oomahs in there. The sprinks'll sprink. Now we just wait."

My pain localized, held a meeting in my forehead. For easement, I popped in my brother's only tape. Johnny Cash sang "I Walk the Line." Jesus. I flicked to the radio. Some chick sang, "Shouldn't I have this, shouldn't I have all of this and passionate kisses," easy for her to pretend she doesn't have any friends, fricking millionaire chick with guys hanging all over her. She can *afford* to pretend. I realized, maybe right then, that I just can't do it, can't pretend like Smarm and Rich Talented Radio Lady. I just say what's really there. Dairy Dreams. Lost Berry Picks. God*damn*.

I flicked some more and got a preacher, then some black music, then I flipped the damn tape back on. *I find it very, very easy*, sang Cash. At least Cash was being honest, you know? Smarm sang with a funny deep voice, and then I grabbed trusty banjo from the back and accompanied all, hwang, hwang, just plucking random chords to keep time. *Because you're mine, I walk the line.* Fun and easing it began to be, like we were seven again, like we were clean, and I was able to forget some of the pain, and I merged with dark green night, and *chick-a-chick-a-chick* simple song, and floating floodlights misty on the granite Peace Tower, and the rows of peaceful cooperative alfalfa, and I allowed myself to pretend that I was clean.

But then Cash was singing another song, slow, with spoken parts. *When Mother used to call from the back steps of the old home place, "come on home now son, it's suppertime."* Corny. Cash's voice cracked, even he thought it was corny.

But me, damn it, I was split wide open to the night and so also to this corny song. Don't ask me why. Sometimes I'm like that, every once in a while something hits me that I can't make fun of, something reminds me that I don't really want to be what I am. *Come home, come home, it's suppertime. The shadows lengthen fast.* I couldn't shut to it. I visioned a back porch bathed in bottley green, with homesome faces nowhere peering, they should have known me but didn't. I wanted Cash to stop the spoken part, because I was scared of the things I was seeing and could hardly breathe. But he didn't stop, and then he was moaning, *Someday we'll all be called together 'round the great supper table up there, for the greatest suppertime of them all, with our Lord. I can almost hear the call now. "Come on home, son. It's suppertime, son."* Lord was reddish as he called me, me too afraid to answer. I don't believe in God, but some kind of Lord was there. Wasn't Jesus.

Then Cash faded out, and I was made aware of Smarm, tube-sniffing by my side. He'd been long quiet, too. I knew he'd been troubled and nailed by some of the same stuff as me, knew he'd also felt Lord gleaming through. So we could only sit in silence, me and Smarm and Lord in silence of hissing end-of-tape.

Then Smarm said, "Johnny Cash is a faggot old man, shit," and he flicked the silence off.

I said, "Fuck, Smarm!" and wanted to tell him he was a hypo-prick and remind him that the Indians hated him and that he was as white as the rest of us and that he was smelly and boring, and I started to get the words together,

but I then saw a purplish light pierce the green night, the front chapel door opening, then heard a screaming nighthawk or buzzer, a buzzer, an alarm, then a puff of black smoke and a smell of the insides of stomachs poofing from the chapel, followed by multi-colored people pouring out. Smarm said, "Yeah, baby, everything worked just right!" and we watched as they all jogged and gagged and stumbled by, drenched, plaid, checkered people, a kid in a fishing hat, a Mickey Mouse ears, a bent one in a wheelchair. And it was revealed to me that there was nothing wrong with these people. I mean I'm sure there was lots wrong, but I didn't know what it was, so I'd better leave them alone. But it was too late, I'd already ruined a hundred vacations. So I didn't cackle with Smarm.

I don't believe in God or Jesus, they're just another cow-crap pose for the rapists and the rest of them. But I do think of that night, and how it's not really that hard to walk the goddamn line, and how I do wish I were clean again.

Apprentice

"Never write a story about writing," G. F. informs Baby Laura. It's the fifth class meeting, the end of the first week. He's unbuttoned at the top now, and his hangover is admirably subtle. "It's a sign of immaturity. Better learn that now, while you're still in high school, right? Now *some* people can pull it off, okay, say, Barth, but. . . ."

Baby's face is scrunched, the lips pulled tight, and she's squeezing her hands together, fingertips turning red. Kind G. F. decides to rescue her. "Okay, look, kiddo, you've got some good stuff here, but my point is, your readers are just going to think you're whining. You know, 'Oh, I'm a tortured writer,' all of that. People don't want to hear that. You should—hey! You should come up with a *metaphor* about writing, yeah." He nods, genuinely excited for three seconds, but then reverts to his smirk: fine, strong jaw thrusting down to the left, lip corners disappearing. Baby misses the smirk, though, because she's unclasped her hands and is taking notes, a good little student lapping up the expert advice.

I'm twenty-four years old as I sit in the midst of these summer-prep-school teens. I'm privileged to be G. F. Benet's apprentice.

G. F. tells me there's a *rich tradition* of novice writers apprenticing the masters. But if some god walked into this classroom and said to me, "Melanie, I'm going to make you write just like G. F. Benet, make you *be* like him," what would I say?

"Metaphor, right. It's the *blood* of good writing," says G. F., smirking and puffing in the light shafts. I guess the smirk is supposed to let us in on the joke. I don't think any of us get it. At least I don't. But I'm in proper awe of him, so I don't ask him to explain. I need to find *something* to say, though, some contribution. The apprentice shouldn't be a cipher, I assume.

"So if you don't learn anything else this summer," he continues, "learn that. All right? I've been writing for twenty years, and that's the most important thing I can tell you." Smirk. "Metaphor powers everything. It *intoxicates*." Smirk smirk. "True metaphor. Without it, uh. . . ."

"Without it, we're lost!" I guess.

But nothing mixes these days. Through the blinds and out of the air conditioner stream more shafts to stripe the kiddies, bending their noses and cheeks, piercing G. F. in the chest, daring me to look at him as he glares, pissed at my intervention. I shrink and look instead to Little Lenny from New York. He's sixteen and parched. A piece of green floss trails out of a corner of his pale mouth. I know I should be soaking up G. F., like a good little apprentice, but he's only a rhythm now, da-da-*duh*, da-da-*duh*, NPR-like, no meaning for me. Lenny, now, there's *living* metaphor, I mean, *mint floss*, that must mean something.

***

G. F. gives three readings each summer session, in the Alumni Room. This year, at the first one, he recites from his latest collection: *Where It Happened*. He reads, "The fat girl got off the sofa in a hurry. In a *fever*. Harrison took another sip of his beer." The audience laughs knowingly at this. I can't follow the story or the joke, but their entranced faces attest that he's in total metaphoric control, and that we're blessed by his presence.

I try to figure out how he pulls it all off. I write in my blue apprentice notebook, *Short sentences. Juxtaposition. Impressive.* But in the margins I find myself scratching crucifixes through the paper. An immature, jealous display, for I have here also an article from the *New York Times*, entitled "A Master of Subtlety": *His stories are emotionally precise, technically brilliant. Benet is, quite simply, one of the finest practitioners of the craft.*

"It was on a package of rubber cement," I hear him saying to Sarah the French Teacher after the reading. "*Harmful if Swallowed*, you know." They both emit risqué laughs and shake their heads. I'm standing to the side, attentive, dutiful little apprentice. "The whole story came out of that. The whole *collection* did, it's all about that."

I've no idea what he's talking about. I tried to read a couple of his stories when I got this job, and I didn't discern that they were about swallowing. I must learn to discern stuff like that. In college, back home in Illinois, I attended lectures and wrote papers on, to name two, Wharton and Melville, both of whom lived just down Route 7 from here, in Massachusetts. Seemed important then, but none of it is helping me to decipher G. F. and his particular brand of metaphor and beer.

After the reading breaks up, the faculty party rages while I drive up Route 7 to Rutland, where I'm small and comfortable at a crumbling shrine shaped like the food pyramid, though topped not with fats but rather with bleeding, thorny Christ-on-a-cross. Metaphor? I've no idea.

Next day, during class break, G. F. guides me with an insistent finger to the Class of '17 alcove. There's just a hint of beer mixed in with his cologne, quite subtle.

"Why weren't you at my party last night?"

"Huh? Oh, I took a ride up to Rutland."

"What?"

"I took a ride up to Rutland. To this shrine, uh—"

"Why? Why didn't you come to the party?"

"I don't like parties. And I don't drink anymore, so. . . ."

He shakes his head of loose curls. "So, what, you get drunk alone? You should have been there. I mean, that's *my* party, and you're the apprentice. . . ." He laughs a bit, lightly incredulous. "I mean, that's so rude, right?"

"Sorry." Tonight of course I won't sleep because I'll be worrying about what I *should* have said to him, how I *could* have explained my clumsy self.

We head back to class so G. F. can continue turning the kids on to the Good News of Ray Carver, this week's featured saint. And most of them are coming around now, they seem to grasp something that I can't even sense. "Carver's got such . . . control," marvels Laura. "Of his metaphors, you know." G. F. nods. After class she tells me, "G. F. was hard on me at first, last week, but I know now it was for my own good."

"Well, that's good, Laura, that's . . . mature," I say, staring at her huge, perfectly sticked lips, and smelling a spritz of something on her, too, I can't quite make it out, her own subtlety mixed in with her classy perfume. Last week she smelled like bubble gum. Now she's maturing under G. F.'s tutelage, learning to be precise, blossoming under him, a subtle little miracle I'm privileged to witness.

At least Lenny's still stunted, though, so I'm not totally alone. Lenny doesn't see what the big deal is about Carver.

He says he wants to be like Wordsworth, he wants to figure out God. "This is a *fiction* course, Lenny," smirks G. F., accurately. After class he mutters to me, "Shit, that kid Lenny is so pretentious."

"Yeah," I say, "that's true."

**

This summer session was supposed to get me back on career and self-esteem track. Life track. Headmaster Holman called me in April and told me that G. F. had picked me from among a hundred applicants for Stafford's writing apprenticeship.

"*Who* picked me?"

"G. F. Benet!" Given his tone, I figured I'd better not ask who the hell G. F. Benet was, or what the point of my phone interview with Holman had been.

"That's fantastic," I gushed.

Holman himself was impressed with my transcripts, a little concerned about my "reserved demeanor" and mumbly explanations of what I'd done in the two years since graduation, but sure I'd burgeon in the presence of the kindred spirit of a kindred writer, the masterful Benet. "You writers," he said, and laughed knowingly, and I joined in to be polite.

"All you have to do is sit in on his class and correct some of the papers," he continued. "You get a nice room, and you don't even have to monitor a dorm, like the other teaching assistants do. G. F. insists that his apprentice be free of that stuff. He takes a great interest, that's why he picks his apprentice directly instead of having me do it."

"Sounds like a great deal."

"Oh, yeah. For a young writer, it's a wonderful opportunity. And it's been so great for the school, a real catch.

This'll be G. F.'s fifth summer here, and I tell you, we count our blessings that we still have him. After that piece in the *Times*, he could go anywhere. He didn't confirm for this summer until just a few days ago; that's why I didn't mention him when you and I first talked, didn't want to get your hopes up. But we got him! Really, we're blessed."

But it's now two weeks into my summer-of-a-lifetime and all I can do is gag on the countless tales of G. F.'s past mentoring, his past wonderfulness to past apprentices and their inevitable blossoming love for him. What's different about me, what thing makes me hate him?

I mean, he's certainly nice enough to shape the apprentice's life and writing in his valuable free time. He directs me to a dorm stoop and hands me back a story I wrote. I sent it in with my application. After my April conversation with Holman, I assumed that G. F. had read it, but he doesn't seem too familiar with it.

The story's my big success, it took second prize in college. I won twenty bucks and a scarf. It's about a pre-med who pukes in a trough and then smiles for more, and another woman who sits alone at parties and doesn't quite get any of it, weirdo.

"Look, I want to help you, Melanie," G. F. says earnestly, "So I'm not going to bullshit you."

"Good!" says the mature, tough apprentice as her stomach clenches.

"So here's the deal. Your characters are way too self-aware. Self-pitying."

"Ah."

"Too much analysis. A reader doesn't want to hear that. A reader wants *metaphor*. And what's with the run-on sentences? A writer.... look, let's not bullshit, a good writer doesn't *need* tricks like that, okay. Come on, you have to learn the rules before you break them." He chastises my college for not teaching me the definition of sentimentality: "*Unearned emotion.* You have to earn it. Every word has to count, every metaphor has to bead up with another one somewhere in the story. They have to match up, and you have to be subtle about it. You can't just throw them at the wall. I mean, you have to *earn* it, right?"

"Right."

"It's like . . . the same with the way you dress. I mean, why are you always walking around with that goofy UAW cap on?"

"Huh?"

"I mean, I'll do you a favor by telling you—you look like a joke. Wake up, okay, you're in Woodside, Vermont. Quit hiding behind the message. You know, you have nice hair, I saw it in your application photo. So let people see it. With the hat, and the no makeup thing. . . . You don't look *anything* like the picture on the app." He playfully pushes my cap up a bit with a forefinger. Even his hand smells cologned.

I stand immediately, feigning a need to stretch. "I'm a little lost," I dare to say. "I mean, the hat—I just bought it at a rally, I wear it so I don't have to comb my hair. I don't get the connection between it and my story."

He sighs. "The connection is that there's no easy path to good writing, kiddo, just hard work. I mean," smirk, "what, the only way to write it is to write it." He tries to be nice. Yeah. But *tough.* That's his job. I won't benefit otherwise. Baby Laura understands, why can't I?

I'm so lost, it's comical. Nauseous, too—I can picture the cologne swishing about in my empty stomach. Meanwhile Leslie from class is walking past, statuesque at fifteen, hair classily short and gelled. "Hi, G. F.," she giggles.

"Hi, Leslie," he giggles back, mimicking her tone perfectly. She and her friends dissolve into delight over G. F. God am I lost.

He turns back to me. His raised eyebrows seem expectant.

"In college," I bleat, "a few years ago, is when I started to write. I figure that's why I got this apprentice job. Some people at college said they were moved by my stuff. And I figured, you know, you must have liked this story, since it was part of my application—"

"Yeah, well, welcome to the real world, right? But I'm happy to help you. We'll see you, kiddo, we'll see you over at my apartment tomorrow night. We'll work on it, huh? Bring some Heineken." Nice, right? His shirt's billowing a bit in the gentle Vermont breeze, a chest curl or two peek out. Little *c*'s. The way he acts, the way he gets it across. The way all flock to him but me. We'll work on it. I won't go to his apartment tomorrow night, no, no, but we'll work on it, we'll work on the writing.

But now every time I sit down to write, some crap gets in the way. An itch. Some kid's TV blasting a Coors commercial. Don't fall off my wagon. *Off the wagon*, shit, that's not even a metaphor, it's a cliché, even I know that. Now a bug flies by, study it, study it, smash it, goddamn it, I haven't written since I got here. I'm supposed to be blossoming under G. F., but instead my stamen's blackened and can hack forth only rant vials, mixed-up metaphors. I think there was a time when I liked to write. But now G. F.'s voice is blotting all: *Every word has to count. Hard work, kiddo. Let's see your hair. Bring some Heineken*. I haven't been here three weeks and already I'm tossing Vitalize after Vitalize down my gullet, tiny yellow caffeine tabs that keep me dry, and I'm begging for any image, just anything to write, any metaphor. I've got ideas, I've even got plots, but G. F. says I need metaphors.

How about my special apprentice dorm room? Its cleanliness is deceptive: new, flowery wallpaper masking years of scrawled *fuck*'s. And what else, bourgeois potpourri air freshener masking working-class Raid. I try these out on G.F. and he bites his lip, shakes his head, and then says, "No. Come on. Clunky. Clunky metaphor. You know, you know what you need, Melanie, I don't want to be harsh, but you want me to be honest, right?"

"Right!"

"Okay then. You need to get out of the nineteenth century, or wherever you're stuck. The way you dress, the way you write—get away from the Romantics, or whoever. I don't know what the hell you did for four years in college, I mean ... I can't believe you never read Carver." He shakes his curls in wonder at the state of liberal arts. "I mean, you really need to read some more recent stuff." So he nicely gives me the name of a book to buy, *Fifty Great Stories of the Late 90's*, and tells me to make sure to read the foreword, "The Craft of Fiction," and the two pieces by him. I rush to Rutland to get it.

And I'm a diligent apprentice, so I try hard to learn from it, but I get mired in the fawning foreword, more stuff about technical precision, or precise technicalities, I don't know, I find myself back at the shrine at 5 a.m., downing Vitalize and Coke and staring at the crabgrass at the base of the cross. I call G. F. around 7 and spin a tale about my car snapping a belt, and I'm stuck in New York or New Jersey, I'm not sure which, and I can't make class. He's pissed at my calling so early on the morning after a party, and he's baffled by my yarn, "Huh, I don't get it, huh," but he seems relieved that the classroom will be free of my awkward presence for a day.

Free of G. F., I and my stomach loosen momentarily, and I drive randomly for most of the morning. Still loose and somehow finding myself in Connecticut, I decide to make an anti-G. F. statement by merging Romantically with primitive nature on the Appalachian Trail. Okay, so no one will witness the statement, but still.

I spend the next two hours trying to find the damn trail, which twines seductively about Route 7 on the Triple-A map but in reality is nowhere to be found. By late evening I'm back at the shrine.

***

I search the faculty for someone to confide in. It's a weak field. I finally settle on the veteran history teacher Carlton, because someone said he brings four students to rural Kentucky every year to feed the poor. So I figure he has a soul.

"I'm scared of G. F.," I tell him. "I feel like we're from different planets."

"What do you mean?" he says. We're sitting in the woody dining hall near the end of dinner period, and he's winking and nodding at colleagues and students as they file out.

"Well . . . here's an example. The other night, he tells me that I'm dressed like the nineteenth century. I was wearing a baseball cap, t-shirt, and jeans, for Christ's sake. What the hell was he talking about? I mean, is the guy just an idiot, or am I missing something?"

"Slip him some Heineken, and he'll love you," soulful Carlton grins.

I don't reply. Someone said in a meeting that silence is okay at moments like these, so I just walk out and back to my dorm.

But what if people mistake my silence for snobbery? I'm sweating over this and other complexity in the darkness when Little Lenny opens my door and starts vomiting forth pleas for assistance with the epic poem he's composing.

I flip on the light. He's a pleasingly askew kid, his head too big for his frail frame, his glasses crooked. "Lenny," I say, "why don't you go see G. F.? I've seen him spend hours with some of your classmates, and Christ, they walk away glowing."

"No. No, G. F. doesn't analyze poetry, only fiction. And he, uh, I think he likes the girls better, anyway. And also one other thing, you know . . . he's too, say, frightening. Repellent."

"Yeah!" I yell. Lenny stumbles backwards. "What do you mean, though, Lenny? Frightening means different things to different people. Come on, talk," and I smile and pat his weirdly striped tummy to ease him.

"Well, just . . . he says writing's the most important thing in life, right, the most important technical element or something, right? He says nothing else matters. But the thing is, I don't even like his writing."

"Wow. Wow. You know, Lenny, you're a good kid—a good person—and I want to help you with your epic. And maybe we'll be friends, ha ha! But before we start, I was just thinking . . . that this writing thing is bullshit. I mean, if a prick like G. F. is the best there is, then it must be bullshit, right?"

"Well, I don't suppose you have to be a good person to be a good writer."

"Whatever," I snap. I don't like to be contradicted by my potential ally in misery. "In any event, we certainly *should* be . . . feeding the poor. That's obviously a better way to spend one's life, morally."

"Feeding the poor?"

"Yeah, feeding the poor! I mean, not that I'd have the guts to actually do it or anything, but, you know, it's . . . just important to assert. To admit. To what we *should* be doing, regardless of whether we do it." Yes, this makes sense.

Lenny smiles weakly; he's sentimental by nature. He doesn't earn his emotion.

He still wants to write his epic, so I steal a few half-remembered lines from Milton and bequeath them nonchalantly to Lenny, then toss him a couple of Vitalize to cheer him up. By now everyone else is at the weekly dance, where G. F.'s boogying prowess is legendary and which I'm sure Apprentice Etiquette requires me to attend. But Lenny and I stay in my room, playing one-on-one vicious pillow football to a swirling Debussy soundtrack. I Vitalize him further to keep us going.

"Don't tell your parents I'm giving you these, Lenny. I mean they're not illegal or anything, but, you know."

"Yeah!"

"Caffeine sharpens you," I tell him, "not like this other shit," flashing him a faculty-party memo that puts quotation marks around the word *beverages*. "I know the difference between them, believe me, and caffeine sharpens you." Lenny might not know what I'm talking about, but still he smiles.

A couple days later, Carlton's chiseled face appears before me as I'm heading into class. He pulls me into his office, the walls of which are plastered with plaques commemorating his tireless work with the wrestling and debating teams.

"Hey," he says, "I have to tell you, you know, you and this kid Lenny.... You've got to be careful about getting mixed up with students."

"Jesus Christ, I'm not 'mixed up' with him! It's possible for me to hang out with a male without being 'mixed up' with him. *Je*sus." My body's slowly beginning to resist the power of Vitalize, and I'm willing to take the resultant irritation out on the carefully groomed and overrated Carlton.

"Well," he says, scratching a lovingly tended sideburn, "anyway, you should be, you know, hanging with G. F. He doesn't like you skipping out on the dance and stuff."

"Oh, for Christ's sake, this sounds like third grade."

"I'm not kidding! Don't forget how lucky you are to be working with this guy for a summer. I mean, did you see that piece in the *Times*? The apprentice usually.... I mean, come on, it's kind of expected that she'll be with G. F. Or whatever."

Naturally it's not until afterwards in a three-Vitalize moment that I'll realize what Carlton means, a gas-cramp flash will illuminate for me what *being with* G. F. means, being with chest hair and Heineken, with manly writer with manly talent and brilliant technique and emotional precision and what is good and what is bad, and G. F., I'm supposed to be with G. F.

Meantime Carlton gets joshy sincere, saying, "Get with the program, sweetie. You should get with the program."

"No, I joined a different program," I mumble half-heartedly, wondering if I've hit upon a metaphor, but figuring Carlton can't hear me anyway. "For a while back home, in Illinois," in a church basement. Ma's still in Illinois, and she thinks apprenticing a famous person like G. F. is going to *help Melanie get back on track*, so here I am doing so in Vermont, and Dad, who the hell cares, but anyway I don't think of my parents.

Instead, I'm dreaming bits of G. F. He's giving a reading on the school golf course. "The cathedral was empty," he intones. "In the light, she washed her hands." When he says *light*, he illuminates, and humanity nods at his brilliance. When I write *light*, it's too, too it's, too sentimental, unearned, too Romantic, too Latinate. What is it? G. F. says my writing's "too wet and teary." Christ, I thought I was dry. Is that a metaphor? I couldn't nail an original one if you fucking paid me. And I know I need to stay on my wagon, but everyone *says* get off, and there's another cliché, I'm just clinging to the clichéd wagon, crashing along on a rutted track, but the only way I know to stay on it is to keep it moving.

So on my free weekend, I load the wagon with Vitalize and let it drag me to Quebec. Where I joyfully discover Canadian Vitalize, which has an extra ingredient not allowed in the States. The package is printed in French so I don't know what the extra bit is, but at least it snaps me to a different place, and I'm revitalized as I drive back down through upstate New York, and it's nighttime so I don't see the houses, and I can pretend it's all just one black forest, free of people and

Heineken and metaphors. I'm revitalized and able to forget G. F. for a few hours.

Back on campus I find Lenny in his dorm room, sweating from lack of Vitalize. I flick him some Canadian tabs and we're soon bonking empty plastic water jugs off each other's heads and reading easy Blake and Montagu poems. "Don't let anyone tell you this is too sentimental, Lenny. Or too pretentious."

"Okay."

The next day is the Second Reading, at which the apprentice is supposed to introduce the Master. I'm still feeling pretty vital, unable to blink, and reveling a bit in my secret strength. I've got what I want, so I decide to just give the crowd what *it* wants: veneration of G. F. And I find a skirt stuffed in the bottom of a drawer and take my hat off to please G. F. I'll even get my hair done tomorrow, I'll ask Baby Laura where she goes for hers. And I won't feel guilty about any of it, because we'll all be happy in our own unique ways. Easy! Everybody happy!

I stand at the front of a massive wooden room with fireplaces and rare folios on the walls, lightly buzzed faculty packed on couches, fashionably attired students jammed jauntily everywhere, and I say, "It's really an honor to introduce this guy tonight." This phrasing is both deferential and colloquial, and Holman, beloved Headmaster Tequila, smiles fuzzily in his beard. "Our writing students have learned so much from G. F. over the past couple of weeks, but I think I've learned even more. About metaphor. Restraint. Hard work." Technical yet accessible. Appreciative bliss all around. Alive and in control, I sprint for the finish. Furnished with a press release from G. F., I read, "G. F.'s recently been published in *Sperry Review* and *Main Street*." The crowd doesn't react to this, and my legs weaken slightly. These are big-time prestigious mags, it says so right here in the press release, and in the *Times* article. But they're not exactly in this crowd's sphere, and I fear I'm not giving the people what they want. So I lighten things up by identifying with them. "I know, I mean, I hadn't even *heard* of those magazines before this summer, but I know now that they're impressive. Yeah, that's another thing I've learned this summer . . . um, from G. F. . . ."

The air's gone dead. And I've no wit, no metaphors, with which to animate it. They think I'm insulting G. F.

My breath drops out completely, and here's a long arid minute where I can't sound. I can feel G. F.'s heat rising behind me. Somehow I've failed him again. I try to say something about his brilliance with metaphors and how I'm sure that these recent stories serve to illustrate said brilliance, but my mouth's so dry that nothing emits save a weird, low, doggish noise. Finally, one harsh laugh crashes like breaking bottles, and I smile desperately towards it. It's Lenny, balled and grinning in a corner under a spider plant, biting his fingers.

"Anyway," I croak, "please welcome a great writer, G. F. Benet!" This sets forth relieved, resounding applause, one deep throat in the hollowed-out room. They're so thankful that the Awkward One is through and the Master is come.

As G. F. reads, I replay my speech and wonder why I've screwed up again, why I said what I said. And where the hell those words came from, why I can never find the right ones like G. F. I didn't need to justify the frigging magazines; I could have said he'd been published in *Pigshit Journal*, and they still would have worshiped him. Why didn't I *see* that? *What* made me miss it? And I decide that I will leave here, leave here, never come back. They can find another apprentice for the rest of the summer, there's ninety-nine others who'd be more appreciative than selfish Melanie.

Up on the platform, G. F. reads on. I have to sit just to the right of him, facing the audience, trying to hold my face, bladder, and heart parts steady while caffeine and God-knows-what explode inside. I can't help but hear some classic G. F. metaphors, though, some gems of precision. Something about *sloshing*, and now another one about an *apple-shaped ass*, at which faculty and kids get to giggle naughtily. Dispensing brilliance and naughtiness simultaneously, the guy's truly a miracle worker. I see Baby Laura, packed tight and hair freshly fried, grinning at her younger, messier friends—see what joys await you next summer, if G. F. accepts you for his class? And you won't have to put up with the weird butchy bitch, he'll definitely get a normal apprentice next year.

After the massive standing O dies down and the kids file out, Headmaster Ron announces, "Faculty, remember we'll be reconvening for the party in about twenty minutes. There'll be brownies, cake, and some . . . libations, shall we say?" Hearty roar. Eliot from Dartmouth and Carlton affect extra-deep voices and say "yeah," while I'm standing there with, you know, whirling ring tabs in my stomach, or some metaphor to that effect. But I'm still the dutiful apprentice, so I lurch over and join the line to congratulate G. F.

"Great reading, huh?" some mound of friz says to me. Biology teacher, I think.

"Incredible," I blather. "The guy was just hitting 'em. The metaphors were so . . . evenly spaced. Even the way he sipped his water."

I finally reach him as people are heading over to the party. He won't look at me, choosing instead to finger a folio.

"Great reading, G. F., I mean that's just . . . quite simply it, yeah."

He shakes his head. "That intro was cute, Melanie. Really cute."

"What? I was trying to pay you a compliment, for God's sake! I just . . . I guess I messed it up a little, I got nervous, is that a crime?" My voice is shaking and I can't steady it.

"You threw me so totally off. I mean . . . what is it with you? Haven't I read your stuff? Haven't I tried to be nice to you?"

"Of course!"

"And yet you just throw me totally off. You know, in five summers here I've never had a problem with an apprentice. All the other girls got along fine with me."

"Well, I'm a woman, maybe that's the problem. Ha ha. Just a joke, come on—"

"Never had a problem, not one," he continues. "And now this. What *is* it with you? You come to my reading looking like a wrinkled slob, you, you won't go to my parties, you won't dance with me, won't have a beer with me, won't come over to my apartment, won't. . . . I mean, forget it, just forget it."

"Why," I say, eyes closed, razorworms in my temples, "why did you pick me for this job?"

"Oh, grow up."

"G. F., the reading was fucking brilliant," I manage to say, but I can't get anything else out, because my body is on the verge of deconstructing. Didn't mean to screw up again, but could have tried harder not to, could have tried harder to please G. F., little kid, runaway, misfit, fall off, get into decent college and get good grades but fall off again, then land an apprentice job and climb back on and dry out and yet you still screw up, you still fall off, and you didn't even get any fun out of it this time.

G. F.'s now in the midst of one last congratulatory clump, he's somehow rising and bobbing above the crowd, grinning slightly now, free of me.

I turn to leave, and there's Lenny, pop-eyed, Vitalized. "That's what famous people do," he whispers, pointing to G. F. "I've seen a lot of famous people in Manhattan. At functions and things." He smiles as he sucks on streaky bleeding fingers. "G. F., he's, he's technically, really, technically, he's just, what, an asshole. Apple-shaped."

***

So a couple hours later near the wasted hilly outskirts of Rutland, I tell Lenny that he's missed dorm check-in, and he just cackles like a little madman and yells, "Mercy Pity Peace and Love, Mercy Pity Peace and Love!" But I know that eventually his Vitalize will wear off, and then he'll be pathetic like me.

I pull us into an empty mall parking lot. "What am I going to do with my life, Lenny? I mean, forget the writing thing. I can't even come close to understanding what the hell he's talking about, or laughing about, any of them. And he's the *best*, if I can't understand the best. . . . I don't know how to be what he wants, how to be a writer. I don't even know how to pay him a compliment. And I've been here a month and haven't come up with one goddamn metaphor. I suck. I'm not feeling sorry for myself—it's just a fact. I mean the only way to write it is to write it, right? And I can't even do that." I'm rubbing palm skin off onto the stick shift, anything, any fucking thing.

"Well, um . . . you said we should be feeding the poor, anyway."

I chew however many tabs remain, cheekful of yellow sand, not quite sure what such quantity will do. The first thing it does is cramp me to the point that I jerk over and bounce my head off the steering wheel. "You know, it's not magic, this Vitalize," I squeak. "It's just another drug, not magic." Lenny says I could have fooled him.

After a box of Gas-X, though, everything just goes kind of numb. I'm at equilibrium for a moment, no pain *for real*.

I've no idea how long or what will last, so I just keep us moving, driving rapidly to a Subway shop and then to the shrine.

"It's hard to find the poor out here, Lenny. But I know they're here, I saw statistics in the paper. Not everyone in Vermont is rich, or goes to prep schools."

We lay the subs out on a black plastic platter by the foot of the shrine steps and then lie back in the car. Outside, a cat slinks up and sniffs the platter. "Probably attracted to the tuna," says Lenny. His lopsided head gets rested on my shoulder, and I let it stay there.

After a long time some pigeons drop down and fight with the cat. My stomach begins to inflate and deflate of its own accord.

"This isn't working, it's not helping," I say. Lenny's asleep, wheezing softly. My body's not mine, the organs, the liverish things, they're like rubber, all these parts inside, and I don't know what else to ingest to help me, except for the one thing I can't take. It's maybe dawn.

Through the grime a round, faded, blue lady walks up to the shrine, her hands in the pocket of her overcoat in August, her face pinched for morning prayers.

Lenny's awake and pointing, the lady's leaning down to the sub pile and maybe takes one, maybe something happens, maybe a metaphor, maybe even an epiphany, because Lenny says "yes" and pats me but I'm shivering, and my breath and face are breaking, and my mouth's full of my stomach, and G.F.'s holding court in his Heineken pool, and all of me breaks open and Dad washes in on his warm can of Ballantine, which he preferred, jammed and rattling between driver's seat and door as we weaved the Tollway on our way home from Wrigley, early seventh-inning exit to catch Regal Wine and Spirits before they closed at five, and Ma preferred other things, a rotten fruity smell and getting home from work and just not being Ma, I preferred, I prefer, still, who I am, because it turns out that they're all the fucking same after all, imbecilic middle-class sloshed parents and famous drunken groping writer, turns out I could have apprenticed my goddamn parents and gotten as much out of it, and I don't want to be like any of them, because I prefer Vitalize, right now, but it wears me to the rubber, and I'm terrified that I'll soon say screw it and find another Regal on some Rutland corner, and that will end my story for good, and G. F. says he reads the ends of stories first because that's what Carver or some such stud taught him to do, well okay hi there, you're a hero, you've changed lives with your writing and self and dick, got written up in the *New York Times*, you're justified and I'm not, I admit it all, but oh let me die at my dashboard before I say yeah, godhead, make me be like G. F. Benet.

So I can't write. Okay. I don't write. I can't be with G. F. What the Christ do I do.

But Lenny's shining next to me, eyeballing the lady, snapping red his fingers and giggling. "Yeah, we fed the poor, all right! What next? What's next, Melanie?"

***

Would You Like to Read More of Matt's Work?

If you enjoy this book and would like to be informed of Matt's future releases, please e-mail him at md89@post.harvard.edu. Thanks for your interest!

Printed in the United States
111860LV00001B/142/A